The Smallest Room

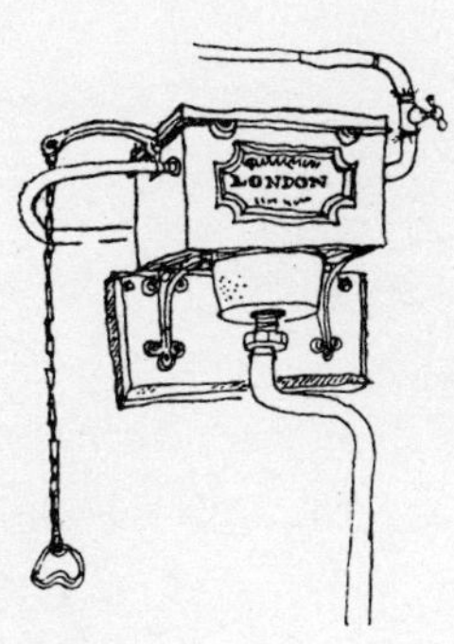

The Smallest Room

John Pudney

Decorations by

DAVID KNIGHT

ALAN SUTTON
1984

Alan Sutton Publishing Limited
17a Brunswick Road
Gloucester GL1 1HG

First published 1954
This edition published 1984

British Library Cataloguing in Publication Data

Pudney, John
The smallest room.
1. Water-closets—Anecdotes, facetiae, satire, etc.
2. Privies—Anecdotes, facetiae, satire, etc.
I. Title
696′.182 TH6498

ISBN 0-86299-133-1

Printed and bound in Great Britain by
The Guernsey Press Company Limited,
Guernsey, Channel Islands.

For

HELEN AND WILLIAM LAIDLAW

whose efforts in furnishing
thoughts, guidance and suggestions
for this, my Smallest Room,
have been so untiring,
and, for me, rewarding

Acknowledgment

THE AUTHOR IS GREATLY INDEBTED TO MR. WILFRED Hanchant for his scholarship and research work: to members of a club whose motto is *Sodalitas Convivium*: to the staff of The Royal Sanitary Institute: to the Editor of *The Architectural Review* and many of his readers: and to members of the various trades connected with his subject. Correspondents in Britain, in U.S.A., and in many European countries have been most generous. Space does not permit recognition of them all and it would seem invidious, and perhaps not even welcome, to single out individuals. To Mr. C. Hamilton Ellis, the author is particularly grateful for generous advice upon everything concerning railways. The author owes a great debt to the many plumbers whom he has been fortunate enough to meet in many places whose character and integrity have contributed to the entirely fictitious character of the Mr. Fleet who is to be found in these pages. Acknowledgment is made to all concerned for extracts used from the following books:

Global Mission by General Arnold (Hutchinson)
Fred of Oxford by Fred Bickerton (Evans)
Bull of Minos by Leonard Cottrell (Evans)
Palace of Minos by Sir Arthur Evans (Macmillan)
Occupation: Writer by Robert Graves (Cassell)
Ross and the New Yorker by Dale Kramer (Gollancz)
Period Piece by Gwen Raverat (Faber)
Cleanliness and Godliness by Reginald Reynolds (George Allen and Unwin)
Building in England Down to 1540 by L. F. Salzman, F.S.A. (Oxford University Press)
Always the Young Strangers by Carl Sandburg (Cape)
Portrait of a Young Dog by Dylan Thomas (Dent)
Mrs. Astor's Horse by Stanley Walker (Bodley Head)

and from an article:

The Craft of the Coffer Maker by R. W. Symonds (*The Connoisseur*)

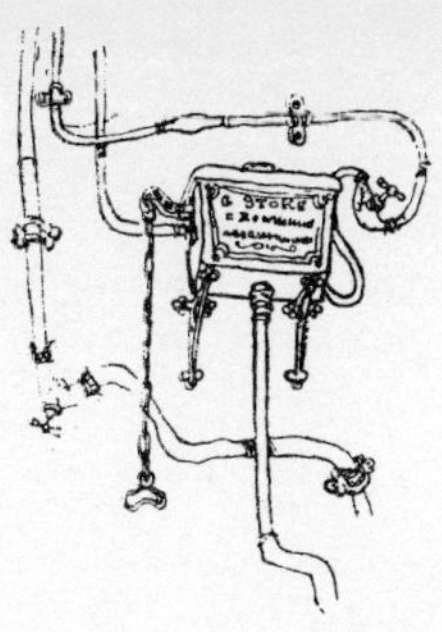

Contents

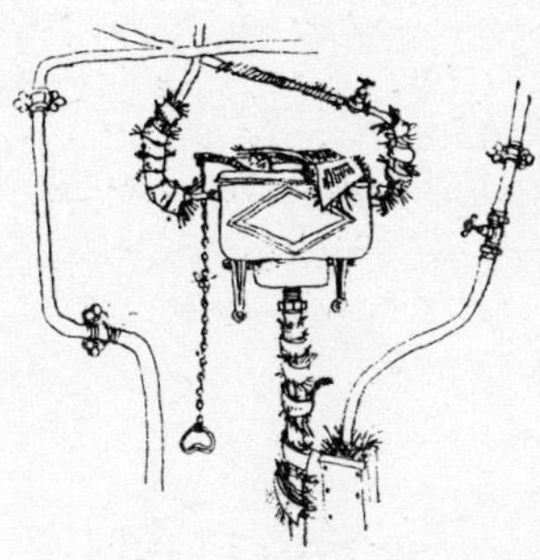

On building a smallest room

INTRODUCING OUR OWN SMALLEST ROOM IN ITS EARLIER STAGES—MR. FLEET, THE PLUMBER—THE REASONS FOR WRITING THIS BOOK

THE new smallest room attached itself to our household almost by chance. A corner of the house was threatening to fall down. The retaining wall of Kentish ragstone, fashioned by village masons a couple of centuries before horse-drawn traffic went out, to support what even then was an old house, bulged and sagged in sudden alarming protest. Village masons took it down, excavated some wooden drains which might have been a Roman tribute to the goddess Cloacina but which belonged, according to them, but to yesterday, and re-built our wall lovingly, declaring that 'not even them jets'll shake her now.'

All danger of that corner of the home tottering into the street below having been averted, Fred, the more talkative of the two masons, scratched an ear and spoke—with native delicacy. 'Not that it's for me to say, but I reckon you could do with a proper convenience atop of her, handy to your back door,' he suggested. 'Nice neat lean-to, you could have: and do away with that there old Jericho. . . .' He nodded toward the obsolete dilapidated place design screened by laurels from the kitchen windows: and the biblical allusion put me in mind of Parson Woodforde, an entry in whose diary for April 26, 1780, was indeed echoed by Fred's very word: 'Busy in painting some boarding in my Wall Garden which was put up to prevent people in the kitchen seeing those who had occasion to go to Jericho.'

Indeed the good parson's Jericho, like ours in its heyday, accommodated more than one, for he records a puzzling circumstance in December 1769: 'Jenny and the maid being at the Little House, some person or another came to the door of it and rapped against it three times with a stick. What it means I know not.'

Fred, the mason, recalled me from my reverie of eighteenth-century Norfolk. 'Proper eyesore is that old Jericho. . . . Now with a lean-to built of rag and set atop of the wall. . . .'

'I shall use it as a tool shed, Fred. I wouldn't dream of having it pulled down. . . .'

Fred scratched his ear again. 'There's no accounting for tastes,' he murmured. 'She ain't built of nothing but old rotten timbers and plaster and such.'

'So you'd side with the Local Authorities and have it down, I suppose?' I suggested.

'Side with *them*? Why I'd sooner see that little old Jericho done up as a real fancy flusher. But you're going to have your work cut out to keep the right side of the Local Authorities when we puts up the new one atop of the wall.'

A bare twenty-one miles away from the centre of London we live. Yet, having been talked into building the new closet, we became the talk of the place—or rather our smallest room did. Its northern wall, above the street for all to see (for we live on a hill), is a masterly example of the stonemason's craft, its façade at least somewhat reluctantly passed by the Local Authority, thus denying Fred the luxury of outraged protest against authoritarian belittlement of his masonry. That wall, its pattern and texture blending with that of the house built, no doubt, by Fred's distant ancestors, was to be the really exceptional feature of an otherwise undistinguished lean-to. There was not enough ragstone for the other two walls, and Fred, his *tour-de-force* upon the public side completed, was content to leave the rest of the job to bricklayers, plasterers, painter and, of course, plumber. We let them take their time in considering all this and then we took ours. We luxuriated in telling the plumber, when he pointed out *à propos* of nothing that Rome was not built in a day, that we were in no hurry. This was not, after all, our only smallest room. Our needs were not pressing. Like the Romans, we could give the matter thought.

'Don't reckon they worried much.'

'Worried? Why, Mr. Fleet'—such is the plumber's name—'they worshipped Venus Cloacina, goddess of the sewers. Her statue was found in a sort of main drain, the Cloaca Maxima.'

Mr. Fleet shuddered. 'What a lark, eh?' Then, to bring us back to the problems of the present, he remarked with rather heavy jocoseness. 'No such things as licences and town and country planning for them heathens, eh?'

'But they had to get a licence to build a privy, in fact, Mr. Fleet. It's mentioned somewhere by Sir John Harington.'

'Talk about the march of progress, eh?' said he, ignoring defeat. 'Now what was that about your wanting a wooden seat? They're gone out of date, you know. You want plastic. That's what you want.'

For no particularly good reason, except possibly a sense of tradition or childhood association, we insisted upon wood, wood painted white, and we said so and added that we did not mind waiting.

'That's all wrong—leastways for people like you who can afford to run two of these places.'

We pointed out to Mr. Fleet first that we never had been able to afford this second smallest room and were indeed talked into it before realizing the expense involved. We took the opportunity, too, to make the mildest of attacks upon Mr. Fleet's well-

known and never very veiled theories of class warfare by recalling an interview with a former Minister of Health, Aneurin Bevan, who not only discoursed sweetly about poetry, of which he is a keen amateur, but stated (for us to print) that the housing of the working classes would no longer be an issue in Britain after his first term of office as Minister, and moreover the said Nye pointed out—and this is where we hit hard at Mr. Fleet—that every working man's house would have *two* smallest rooms, one up, one down.

'Quite right too,' said Mr. Fleet imperturbably, '*with* plastic seats. Now, plastic . . .'

Mr. Fleet on the subject of plastic speaks with an eloquence equalling that of James Boswell describing the quilted seats of a sybarite diplomat of his day. Would I could have summoned a little of Samuel Johnson's forthrightness when he cried: 'No, sir. there is nothing so good as the plain board.'

Yet obstinacy triumphed and it was almost a scuppered Fleet who, not without long delay, set about ordering an inferior white wooden seat. Many months later, the newest, smallest room, decent, demure—created at minimum cost with maximum disputation, almost fortuitously to garnish the top of the new retaining wall—awaited its inaugural ceremony. Fred, the stonemason, alone was proud. Mr. Fleet, in the social security of a prefix used, it is said, even by his wife (who has no knowledge of any Christian name) may have been a wiser if not a better man. The rest of mankind seemed indifferent. Perhaps because it faced north; perhaps because it so conveniently upheld the contemporary doctrine of fitness for purpose; perhaps because of its effulgent newness, this smallest room seemed at the outset chilly, demurely woebegone, lacking in character. Its casual, somewhat controversial, attachment to the household, however, stimulated me to attempt to re-assess the status of the closet in the free world. My newest smallest room should be related to history; garnished by legend, warmed by anecdote, decorated by the pruderies, coynesses and social evasions which bring a sense of adventure to such small places. My pages, therefore, are dedicated to the enrichment of the smallest room. They are offered to such fellow-citizens as regard these places not as mere cells for shameful self-effacement, but as shrines of common-sense and even pleasure—pleasure, it is ventured to hope, these pages may in some wise augment.

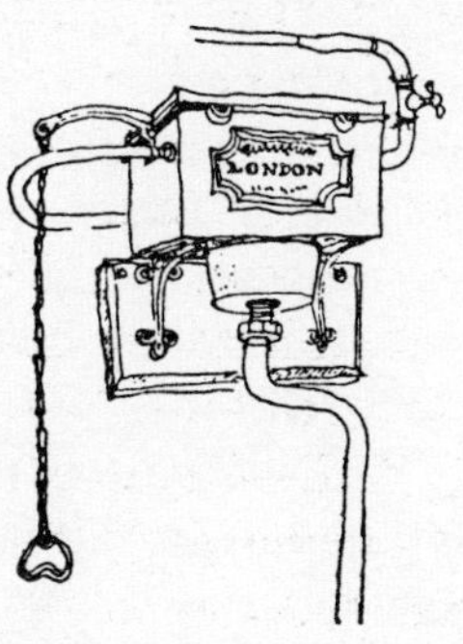

Words for it

TABOO AND RETICENCE—COYNESS AND THE PRINTED WORD—INTERNATIONAL POLITENESSES—EUPHEMISMS FOR THE SMALLEST ROOM AND WHAT TAKES PLACE THERE—THE POPULARITY OF DIMINUTIVES

WHILE studying *Poetical Intoxication* by William Nickerson Bates (for purposes unconnected with this book), I came across a detail of literary technique which might well serve as my text for this chapter. . . . 'And J. K. Huysmans had a preference, when composing, for that indispensable room, so necessary to a happy household but seldom designated in public by name.'

Why so seldom? Why indeed is this *taboo* so universal? Reginald Reynolds, in his comprehensive and entertaining work *Cleanliness and Godliness*, distinguishes between the *taboo* of the Unmentionable and the *taboo* of the Unclean—a nice point, though I fail to see why he confines reticence to Anglo-Saxons. 'The *taboo* against dirt and against uncleanly habits belongs, as we have seen, to all time and to all portions of the globe. But there is a secondary *taboo* that would appear to be peculiarly Puritan in origin, and for this reason of a specifically Anglo-Saxon character, a *taboo* found principally in Britain and in the United States of America, not against dirt itself or filthy habits, but *against any mention of things relating to excretion*. Thus the writing of this book is a breach of this particular *taboo* because society conspires to pretend that the principal objects of discussion do not exist.'

Taboos lead the least likely people to the oddest extremes of delicacy. During the construction of our smallest room, Fred the mason would move off towards the laurels with the incredible statement that he felt he could *pick a daisy*. This was nothing to the arch explanation overheard more than once from the pessimistic lips of Mr. Fleet, whom not even his enemies would describe as sallow-complexioned, that he had had to *powder his nose*.

Robert Graves, exploring *taboos* in *Occupation Writer*, prophesied that some historian of the future might write of our own times: 'Shortly before the

"Great War for Civilization" . . . there was a student at Oxford University famous for his "practical joking" and for deriding the most sacred *taboos* of his time. It was he who first defiled a local altar, "The Martyrs' Memorial," by climbing to its very summit at night-time and planting a chamber-pot—a stringently *tabooed* vessel—on the cross that crowned it. The civic authorities had great difficulty in removing this scandalous object, because climbing the Memorial was no easy feat, and the chamber-pot, being made of enamel-ware rather than, as was first thought, of porcelain, could not be dislodged by rifle fire.[1] . . .

'Even in our enlightened times, the sex- and lavatory-*taboos* linger to a certain extent, owing to the natural reserve that men and women feel about these functions. The lavatory *taboo* survives with us at meal-times, but we find it difficult to understand the extraordinary customs to which the morbid enlargement of this natural reserve led. For instance, the playwright Hogg records that not only was it considered obscene for a man to show a woman the way to a lavatory, but that even man to man or woman to woman, evasive phrases had to be used: "Would you care to wash your hands?" "Have you been shown the geography of the house?" A drunken man is said to have asked his partner at a public dance: "Where is the lavatory?" to which she replied,

[1] This intrepid adventurer climbed the seventy-five foot high Memorial on the night of November 5, 1923, in his stockinged feet and with the aid of an alpenstock, and cemented the pot to the top. It is said that he was fined thirty pounds by his college authorities and that the amount was raised by undergraduate subscription.

disengaging herself: "On the right of the entrance hall you will find a door with the notice GENTLEMEN. Disregard the warning, go right in; and you will find what you want." This was held to be a very correct reply. Nor would even intimate friends consent to notice each other if one of them was emerging from the lavatory or entering it; and, if this was the first meeting of the day, they would greet each other half a minute later on *untabooed* ground with every pretence of novelty and surprise . . .'

I encountered some modest evidence of journalistic *taboo*, in assembling this chapter. I submitted a brief, inoffensively-worded advertisement appealing for information to a newspaper at all times of broad views and high repute. This, however, met with polite but unequivocal rejection: mine was an advertisement the nature of which the newspaper preferred not to accept.

I wonder if a neurotic reticence about the calls of nature mingles with the printers' ink that is said to run in the veins of the panjandrums of journalism. In his masterly account of Ross, the famous editor of the *New Yorker*, Dale Kramer both offers us the current American euphemism *rest room* (the Newfoundland for which is *comfort room*) and also hints at there being a shadow of truth in my theory: 'Women on the staff continued to pain Ross. One of the things that bothered him was the location of the ladies' rest-room. To get to the men's room, it had to be passed. A lady coming out might see Ross marching by, stony countenance firmly to the front. He spent hours trying to devise a way to build separate passages to the rest rooms. He never accomplished it.'

Further evidence of the great Ross's application of this keenly felt *taboo* comes later in the book: 'Ross . . . troubled himself, now that he could afford to, with getting the advertising matter into a companionable relationship with the text . . . the sensibilities of aesthetic readers should be taken into consideration. . . . Deodorants, laxatives (including yeast) and bathroom accessories were declared out of bounds.'

British newspapers too can be vigilantly coy about the advertisements they carry. A lady of my acquaintance who works for a firm of sanitary potters whose name is to be encountered in smallest rooms throughout the civilized world, noticed that a London store was advertising lavatories as wash basins and water closets as toilet basins. Agitated by such abstruse refinement, she wrote to the store for an explanation. The store, whose name is by no means confined to smallest rooms, denied that their own advertisement department had 'become all refined.' They defended the complexity of their language by saying that they had been advised by the newspaper that in future the word *lavatory* in any connection would not be allowed to be used in advertisements.

As an example of the delicacy which advertisers must employ not only in words but in pictures, let me quote extracts from the robust comments of the Advertisement Critic in the *World's Press News*: 'Harpic has been selling on the same sales story since long before the war. Harpic, the name now permanently associated with the smallest room in the house (to borrow an advertising phrase!), invented a great sales idea—and have stuck to it throughout their advertising life . . .

'I'm pretty certain that no other advertiser of any vaguely similar product would be allowed to steal such an individual (and clever) idea as the famous Harpic "Reaches right round the bend in the pipe."

'Other products may do so. Other products may try to evolve a story that says the same thing. But they cannot possibly pinch that fine selling angle.

'To-day, however, the Harpic advertising is very much preoccupied with doing tricks to show the reader *inside* the lavatory without actually going inside it! That is to say, they show the door ajar, the tin of Harpic clearly seen, the lavatory just out of sight. Maybe the advertisement directors of the women's magazines consider the housewife too delicate ever to be allowed to glance into someone else's smallest room!'

The preference of J. K. Huysmans, however, is not uncommon. In certain mountain villages in central Bulgaria, for instance, they speak not of going to Jericho (though that biblical expression always seems to imply a journey outdoors) but of going to the *thinking place.* Thence they derive the euphemisms for one who is so engaged as *thinking*, or even *writing*.

Venturing a little deeper into Bulgarian lore, we find that the schoolboy word for the place for the big need is *west;* and that for the lesser one is *north.* These terms derive from practical hygiene, the conveniences being built respectively to the west and the north of the school buildings in order to avoid the force of the morning and noon sun. For the same reasons, the phrase *shady-place* has a certain polite currency in Balkan countries.

Contemporary adolescence in Britain seems contaminated by the genteel school-marmism *to be excused*. Hence the table-talk bandied about in our homes.

'Have you been excused to-day?'

'He was excused three times yesterday!'

'What do the sentries do when they want to be excused at Buckingham Palace, Daddy?'

'There was no place to be excused at the meeting, so we . . .'

I take these phrases not from hearsay but from recent experience. Not all of them were spoken by children. The please-teacher complex is now deeply ingrained in our way of life. Hearing us talk like this, a visitor from Mars might well regard the English-speaking peoples as being prone to hold up an excusatory hand at any moment. In Parliament, in Congress, in church, at dinner parties, board meetings, or even on the parade ground. On Danish parade grounds, it appears that soldiers, in fact, do. For there is a polite Danish expression used both in military and civilian life: *Ma jeg traede af pa naturere vagne*, which, I am told, means 'May I fall out on behalf of Nature?'

Coyness in these matters undoubtedly stems from that moment in infancy when we are taught not to be actually proud of what we have done. The nursery and the classroom provide us with such simpering phrases as 'being excused.' More advanced education introduces a wider choice. There are schoolboy phrases which are coarsely suggestive or descriptive.

With them mingle some honest direct old English but socially shocking words, such as piss and shit—both words embedded in the texture of English literature but, alas, currently used either with a schoolboy smirk or within the most inner secrecy of our lives.

A number of traditional and academic euphemisms of the politest kind accompany adolescence and maturity. Perhaps because my old school in the 'twenties was regarded as rather modern and progressive, the only Greek word we ever learned to use was the somewhat genteel *topos* for the smallest room. This, in my son's time in the 'fifties, had already been corrupted to *tope*. British schools offer a fair variety of useful if undistinguished phrases, besides the traditional *bog* or *bog-house* which are pre-seventeenth century. At Marlborough College you go *to the woods*, at Lancing *to the groves*, at Winchester *to the forakers*, at Felsted to the *shants* or the *wasses*, and at Leys School, Cambridge, *the Styx*. Gamesman S. Potter, upon whom I have unsuccessfully urged the necessity of writing a work of smallest-roommanship, tells me of the Westminster jargon *going up japs*. From this comes the word *japping*, which, according to the Gamesman, is so obscure to those unlucky enough not to have been at Westminster that it may be used with propriety in any mixed company.

Also conveniently obscure to the uninitiated or to those without the benefit of education at Christ's College, Cambridge, is the phrase *keeping a fourth*, for the interpretation of which I am indebted to two distinguished novelists, C. P. Snow and William Cooper, who explain that the college has but three courts, and the smallest room is held in honour as the fourth. From it derives the undergraduate abbreviation sometimes to be found as a notice pinned to the door of a room in the absence of its owner—*gone 4*. Seats of learning have not been uninventive. There is the Latin-Irish *colfabis* at Trinity College, Dublin. The *Obeum* at Cambridge was reputed to have derived from the initials of Oscar Browning, its ardent propagandist. My own preference is for the now, alas, obsolescent note of gallantry at Brasenose, Oxford, where the latrines were built from funds given by Lady Long and thereafter called *the longs*—surely an unusually imaginative tribute to a benefactress. At least one word of ancient and uncertain derivation, also of uncertain spelling and pronunciation, is shared by seats of learning and houses of correction. At a university, people go in moments of need to the *cuzzes*, which some learned men derive from the Hebrew name of the refuse containers outside the Temple at Jerusalem. In prison people go to a *carzy*, a *cozzy*, or a *karzy*, which other learned men derive from the Hindustani word *khazi*.

Turning to more domestic circles, a polite term universally esteemed on both sides of the Atlantic by people of good family (such as, for instance, the Churchills and the Roosevelts) is *loo*. In my innocence, I had considered this to be but just another *place* euphemism, corrupted from the French *lieu*. The distinguished Wordman, Eric Partridge, more subtly associates it with water. '*Loo*, probably *l'eau*, perhaps

from the Scots' cry *gardy loo!* Look out for the slops—poured from an upstairs window.'

He regards the equally popular *la* as possibly a 'mere variant' of *loo*. With some frivolity, he suggests as an alternative that the French *O là là* might have something to do with it.

Like other nations, the French took both to the word and to the ware in the great Victorian period when Britain was glazing a trail and equipping the smallest rooms of the world. In the four corners of the earth, British culture and civilization effortlessly left its mark in those pre-propaganda days, in the polite, untranslated, variously pronounced but highly prized terms *Water-Closet* and *W.C.* The loyalty of contemporary France to the term is neatly illustrated in this note from Bruce Marshall, who lives in that country: '*Cabinet* is rarely used in France to-day, the popular term being *les vaters*. My daughter's god-father whose name is Waters and who has lived in Paris for thirty years always takes good care to pronounce his name *à l'anglaise*, but even after taking this precaution, he was once referred to as Monsieur Cabinet.'

Several European nations are addicted to telephonic euphemisms. Wing-Commander Yeo Thomas, G.C., recalls that during his parachute visits to France before his capture by the Gestapo, his friends of the Resistance would excuse themselves with the phrase *Je vais téléphoner à Hitler*. Naturally this did not go unaccompanied by Gallic gestures—described by Yeo Thomas as 'pinching one's nose with the fingers of the left hand whilst making the gesture of pulling the chain with the right hand; perfect artists at the same time blew a raspberry to accentuate the meaning.'

The Danes have elaborated the polite excuse of seeking an imaginary telephone with the Viking coyness: *Hvor er Dametelefonen?* which means literally 'Where is the lady-phone?'

The true Briton frequently confuses his foreign guest by inquiring somewhat apologetically whether he wishes to *wash his hands*. When the guest declares boldly, even indignantly, that he is not dirty, social embarrassment is alleviated by an invitation to *use the cloakroom*—to which a really stolid Oriental will inevitably reply that he has no cloak.

We may take some comfort, however, in the fact that diffidence, shyness and even shame in speaking of our smallest rooms appears to be not only international but timeless. The very word cloakroom is but the genteel offspring of *garderobe*, a polite term for the place in the Middle Ages. It meant strictly a place where clothes were kept, but there is abundant evidence that this was synonymous with the smallest room. L. F. Salzman in *Building in England Down to 1540* quotes early uses of the word. At York Castle, for instance, in the reign of Edward III, ten shillings was paid 'for making the pit of the garderobe of the Exchequer.' Then we find in a description of the works of Prior Thomas Chittenden (1390–1411) at Canterbury: 'Also the prior's bed, with a new study and hall above, and a garderobe practically rebuilt and leaded.'

Smallest rooms, by whatever name, were a luxury of the royal, the noble, the rich, or the well-organized in the Middle Ages. Centuries later, man—and woman—often when need arose took to the open air as a matter of course and, in the case of Samuel Pepys, made no fuss about either word or deed: '. . . After dinner, with Sir W. Pen, my wife, and Mary Batelier to the Duke of York's house, and there saw "Heraclius" which is a good play; . . . My wife was ill and so I was forced to go out of the house with her to Lincoln's Inn walks, and there in a corner she did her business, and was by and by well, and so into the house again, but sick of their real acting. So home . . .'

I mention the well-organized because I have in mind the Church which, long before Pepys, was at once well-equipped, capable of coyness, and given to polite terms, the popular ones being the *necessarium*, *necessary house*, or simply *the necessary*, not, according to Salzman's learned research, unaccompanied by diffidence or shame. 'At St. Albans we are told of Prior John, who became Abbot in 1396, that he made a stone cistern in which to store rain-water "so as to cleanse the filth of the convent latrine . . . and he built the necessary house, commonly called the privy dormitory, than which none can be found more beautiful or more sumptuous." He also built a prior's chamber: "but because the latrine of that chamber seemed to be rather close to the chapel of the guest-house the convent was reported by many to have made a place of retirement at the horns of the altar." His predecessor, Abbot Thomas, made at the abbey's cell of Redburn Priory "a new building, that is to say, a privy dormitory or retiring place for the brethren there, and a latrine for himself, because formerly one building served him and the brethren there, wherefore they were ashamed (*erubescebant*) when they had to go to the necessary in his presence".'

Jakes is a word which seems to have deserted our vocabulary. It was in earlier use but had a particular vogue among the first Elizabethans following the publication of Sir John Harington's *Metamorphosis of Ajax* (1596) to which tribute is paid in another chapter. But among the ancient records quoted by Salzman, there are earlier references. In the Tower of London, for instance, in 1525, carpenters were called upon to erect 'particions otherwyse callyd paper wallys under the said vij chambers to devyde the houses of office, and in every particion there a dore new made, and w^{t}in one of these particions a stole made to a jaques.' At Westminster in 1532, there is mention of 'a doble case sette in a windowe within a jakis in the Ladye Wilshires lodgeings.'

The Latin word *latrina*, still much bandied about among the military as *lats*, has, as *latrine*, a long and useful association with the English language. There are records of work being done at Cambridge Castle in 1295 which included the item 'for 10 deal boards for making a spere in front of the seat of the latrine (*le setle cloace*) of the wardrobe of the hall, 2*s*. 6*d*.'

The word *privy* still lingers upon the lips of a good old-fashioned stonemason such as Fred, who uses it, along with *petty house*, to denote a place of easement outdoors. Mr. Fleet, the plumber, also uses the word, but derisively, saying of some smallest room which is not to his taste, 'She be no better than some durned old privy.' The fact is that the word has come down in the world, a victim to the flushing closet. Yet it has been with us for centuries. In 1296, when most of England went about its business in the open, there was a sense of regal luxury about it. For example, King Henry III ordered for Guildford Castle 'a *privy chamber* to the Queen's garderobe': and even earlier, in 1249, at Woodstock, 'a wardrobe, *privy chamber* and fireplace.'

The commoner polite phrases associated with the smallest rooms in our homes to-day mostly seem to have derived from the middle of the nineteenth century, when the possession of a smallest room within the house ceased to be a matter for wonder, pride, and envy. There is a suggestion both of decency and of remoteness in popular Victorian expressions which still linger, such as *to pay a visit to my uncle*, or *to go and see my aunt*, the latter still being polite currency across the Channel as *chez ma tante.*

Slightly less polite Victorianisms still with us are *to shoot a lion*, which to me always carries the nostalgia of Anglo-Indian Simla; and *to shake hands with an old friend*, which I met in a revived form in World War II as *shaking hands with the bloke I enlisted with.*

In the Britain of the nineteen-fifties, there are precious few uses for a single penny. It will no longer buy a bus ride: nor will a penny stamp carry the humblest missive through the post. Its most potent value now is as a key of entry to a smallest room. Thus it serves as a proud perennial mystery to foreigners. A lady's need of a penny used to be the source of much teetering ribaldry. Now *where do I go to spend a penny?* has become a phrase to be spoken with due solemnity by man, woman or child—to the consternation of visitors from outside the sterling area. To one family at least, the phrase perpetuates a worthy memory. Mr. George Jennings, who describes himself as 'Sanitation Specialist, late of Lambeth,' writes: 'In 1855 an important development took place in world Sanitation by the inception of the Underground Public Convenience which was originated by my Grandfather and some years later he constructed the first of its kind on a vacant space outside the Royal Exchange in the City of London. I might add that the charge of one penny which he instituted soon became a source of revenue to many local authorities, and in spite of changes in monetary values it still remains the standard charge and may perhaps be regarded as a lasting tribute to his memory.'

That tribute stands: with but one exception discovered for me by a Kensington lady visiting Stepney: 'There was the usual row of penny-in-the-slot cubicles common to all women's public lavatories, but opposite was a row of cubicles with double swing doors (unlockable) labelled "Urinettes—½d." They each contained a pedestal W.C. without a seat and flushed automatically at intervals. I spoke about them to the attendant but she couldn't understand my interest; it seems that she has held her salubrious job for 27 years and the "urinettes" have always been there, so they are not an innovation.'

Irrelevant though this may be to our present subject, the diminutive, in Stepney used in a severely practical context, has the widest currency in all languages for the purposes of polite euphemism, sharing favour with downright baby talk. *Little boys'* and *little girls'* are found wherever English is spoken. Billy Butlin graces his holiday camps with characteristically zestful notices which read simply *Lasses* and *Lads*. In South Africa, strangers are often puzzled by the esoteric variation *P.K.*, which means *Piccanniny Kiaha*, or the smallest house. The soubriquet I have chosen for my title, *The Smallest Room*, has no great claim to ancient usage. It really belongs to that snug period of our more recent history when those in need were no longer forced to walk outdoors. Among its predecessors are the *littlest house* and that demurely hyphened *little-house* upon which Wesley placed some emphasis when in 1769 he advised his followers: 'I particularly desire wherever you have preaching . . . that there may be a little-house.' Thus suggesting that great preachers may not share the inhibitions of great journalists.

The smallest room itself suffers diminution and becomes in some households *The Littlest Room.* Diminutives are not by any means confined to the structure of places. The *wee-wee*, the *widdle*, the *pee-pee*, and the *piddle* still haunt the adult language with childish excuses. Needless to say, Cockney rhyming slang has made good use of these with such phrases as *you and me* and *Jerry Riddle.*

Euphemisms are a constant tax on the ingenuity of civilized man. In Italian hotels they favour the somewhat austere *numero cento.* So, I find, do religious houses in Cyprus. Recently at Stavrovouni, the mountain-top monastery founded by St. Helena and containing I swear less than fifty rooms all told, the Abbot courteously directed me in my need to a door marked *No. 100.* In more extrovert establishments on both sides of the Atlantic, they put up a placard saying *Here it is.* In Spain, when they use *señores* instead of *caballeros*, gentlemen ignorant of Castilian almost always walk into the *señoras* by mistake. The Greeks have a word for it of course. On the Attic plain I encountered an outside place marked *W.C.*

for the benefit of the unlearned but also, for initiates, *ΑΠΟΧΩΡΗΤΗΡΙΟΝ*—a place apart. My prize for the truly esoteric label goes to the American establishment which offers its customers in their need a choice of two doors decorated with the likeness of two breeds of dog. You have to be something of a canine expert, however great your need may be, to tell which of these is *pointer* and which is *setter*.

Water and Earth

OUR JERICHO—A FAMOUS G.I. LETTER—WATER SUPPLIES —VICTORIAN MIDDENS—EARTH CLOSETS—PAILS AND TUBS—THE GOUX SYSTEM—ASHES—LONDON CESS-PITS —WILKIE COLLINS, LONGFELLOW, AND SANDBURG—NIGHTMEN AND GONG FERMORS—SQUATTERS

ROMANTIC visitors have often associated our own relic in the laurels with the days of doublet and hose; and it is usually assumed that Jericho belongs to the distant past. While there are abundant records of waterless closets in more ancient times—and I hope to mention some of them—hundreds of thousands of Jerichos were, in fact, still being mass-produced at the time of my own father's birth, and indeed continued, though he was too modest to be aware of such matters, all the days of his youth. The provision of piped water is still, in the nineteen-fifties, a political issue and a hackling point on the rural hustings of most English-speaking countries. Even in a Welfare State in this age of the common man, the pulling of a chain on the casual assumption that waters will obediently gush forth is mostly an urban privilege not universally extended to rustic communities.

Such a limitation applies to all communities, no matter how sophisticated, not least the highly civilized French. The call of Nature is not necessarily in their eyes a summons to the closet—with or without a water supply.

'*Ou peux-je aller pisser?*' demanded a friend of mine who is a gifted linguist.

'*Mais, monsieur, vous avez toute la France,*' replied an accommodating *gendarme*, his fine wide gesture encompassing all the 207,076 square miles of that fair, and in such matters uninhibited, land.

That water, even when it is abundant, does not always serve an ordained purpose in closets and such places is recalled in the popular, and I suppose quite unauthentic, letter from a mid-Western mother to her G.I. son serving in Europe: 'Pop has got a job, the first since before you were born. What with that and your allowance, we decided to launch out a bit and build the bathroom we've always aimed for. It was finished a week ago. It's a swell job. In one corner is a large kind of tub, a bit bigger than the pig trough. That's for washing all over. On the same side as that is a smaller basin in which you can wash your face and hands. In the other corner is a pedestal arrangement for your feet. First you wash one in it and then you pull a chain and down comes a fresh supply of water for you to wash the other. And that's not all. The firm that sent out the fittings is generous. They sent us a mahogany frame, though they forgot the glass, and we've put this up in the parlour with the enlargement of grandpop's picture in it. They also sent a solid board that makes a swell bread board and several rolls of writing paper. . . .'

Whatever its authenticity, this vivid epistle enjoys continued currency in the United States, for it is now reproduced as text on a greeting card, a copy of which recently reached me from Hollywood.

A more authentic if somewhat melancholy misuse of a flush was reported in *The Times* of August 8, 1862. 'At the Lancaster Assizes, Walter Moore was found guilty of murdering his wife at Black Lane-ends, Keighley, by cutting her throat with a razor. In this instance the convict anticipated his doom by a few hours, committing suicide in the water-closet, by thrusting his head into the pan and letting on the water.' The surprising aspect of this event lies in there having been a sufficient water supply at Lancaster at that period to serve such a purpose.

It is said that in ancient Rome the aqueducts furnished a daily supply of something like 300 gallons a head. In the Britain of the eighteen-eighties, according to a report of the Rivers' Pollution Commissioners, the average supply in London was 40 gallons a head, in Manchester 21 gallons, in Norwich only 14½ gallons, in the manufacturing towns of Lancashire and Yorkshire an average of 16 to 21 gallons. German cities were better equipped. Karlsruhe, for instance, was quoted at 130 gallons, and 'most of the large cities in America have also very ample supplies.' My source of information on this score is Professor F. S. B. François de Chaumont, who, writing in 1883, goes on to point out that the requirements of country cousins need not be extravagant. 'In dwellings in rural districts, so large a supply as is given in many towns is not always required. If there be no system of drainage, and if the closets or privies be on a dry system, then from

16 to 20 gallons will generally suffice, with an addition for animals that may be employed. Thus, a household of five persons, with, say, one horse, would require, in round numbers, about 100 gallons a day; but if there be no water-closets in use, about 120 to 130 gallons.'

At that time, when such names as Twyford, Jennings, Crapper, and Hellyer were becoming household words—in the better class of household throughout the civilized world (so that even the French, as we have noted, borrowed the useful abbreviation *W.C.*)—there was still a lively interest in the manufacture of Jerichos for the industrial workers of Victorian Britain.

Shirley Forster Murphy, Medical Officer of Health to the parish of St. Pancras and Hon. Secretary to the Epidemiological Society, reviewing the situation, put it succinctly thus: 'With the water-carriage system we are able by a flush of water to remove at once from the precincts of the house matter which, from the beginning, is offensive, and which tends to become more so the longer it is retained, unless special precautions be taken, and in almost all towns, for, at any rate, some of the better-class houses, this system is provided, but the great bulk of a population is often obliged to adopt some other method for the disposal of its waste, and this method necessarily includes the retention of effete matter for a varying time upon the premises.'

With Queen Victoria upon the throne and all well in the world, the medieval system of the midden still mingled with the wonders of the age. Nearly two decades after the wonder of the newest water closet had been displayed in great variety at the Great Exhibition of 1851, a medical officer to the Privy Council offered this report on the middens of Birmingham. 'At present it is common to find huge, wet, foetid middens, uncovered, undrained, unemptied, some of them as deep and big as the foundations of an ordinary cottage. Few of them are covered, the inspector of nuisances thinking they are better left open. Many are under workshops where work is done amid stench all the year round, and among swarms of flies in the summer.'

Such middens were, of course, condemned by Murphy, who, writing a couple of decades later, goes on to describe as a 'distinct improvement' the Nottingham midden. This officially approved affair consisted of two privies opening into the same pit with a small door on either side to receive the ashes and garbage of the house. 'The pit, which is cleared once in every three months, is built in cement, is about 80 cubic feet in size, has a rounded bottom and is sunk below the ground; a roof shuts out the rain from above, and opportunity for ventilation is afforded.' This, however, did not 'answer every purpose.' Murphy preferred the more advanced Hull midden because it was almost entirely above the ground, was limited to the 'mere space beneath the seat,' and was readily emptied by the removal of the front. He confessed to there being some difference of opinion as to the efficacy of ashes: 'The distribution of ashes may be accomplished in a variety of ways; two of them have already been mentioned in the descriptions given of the Nottingham and Hull middens, and a third, that in which the seat of the privy is hinged so that it can be raised up and thus admit the ashes, may be also referred to, a plan which is more frequently found in Manchester. Formerly in Salford the same result was attempted, by placing the midden immediately beneath the seat and floor of the closet, and raising the seat so that there was a step in front of it, thus leaving a space between the step and the floor through which the ashes were thrown in. This plan was, however, found to be objectionable, and has since been abandoned.'

His somewhat reserved enthusiasm was earned by a recent invention, '. . . an ingenious arrangement by which the ashes are thrown through an opening in the side or rear wall of the privy on to a sloping board, which conducts them to the screener, or sieve. By the pressure upon the seat which occurs when the closet is in use, the screener receives a motion that separates the fine dust from the cinders, and passes the former into a measurer, whence it is discharged over the soil the moment the pressure is taken off the seat; at the same time the cinders pass over the screen and fall into a pail below, whence they can be removed for subsequent use as fuel.' It is not surprising that Murphy's final words of advice on the midden system is that the privy should not be near a well and that when it was emptied the conveyance of its contents through a dwelling was to be avoided.

Murphy preferred the Nottingham tub to any midden. These officially approved tubs he describes as having been made of oak, well tarred, about 1 foot

4 inches high and costing 2s. 8d. each '. . . the whole cost of a new closet, including locks and everything being £4.' He goes on to explain that the tubs were removed weekly or at shorter intervals 'according to the interests of the case.' Since they were receptacles not only for excreta but for all the solid vegetable refuse of the house, potato peelings and the rest, and for the solid animal refuse, remnants of food, etc., together with all the household ashes, it is to be hoped that the enlightened authorities of Nottingham never stuck out for weekly intervals. At the time of writing, Murphy stated that there were 24,000 of these closets in Nottingham.

Manchester, Salford, and Rochdale went in for pails and what was termed 'the separation of the excreta and fine ash from the other household refuse.' This involved the construction, as part of the privy, of a cinder sifter, a separate compartment for a large refuse pail as well as various openings for the use of the scavengers. The Rochdale pail had a refinement which put it ahead of the others, 'known as Harescaugh's patent spring-lid receptacle, the lid of which is provided with a cushion of india-rubber which is fastened down by a strong spring.' In Rochdale, every pail, after being emptied, was washed with a hose at 40 lbs. pressure, as well as being disinfected, and the medical officer of health of the day declared that the Rochdale pail had produced a marked improvement in the health of the citizens.

By far the most complicated movable receptacle for privies, devised by Victorian genius, was the Goux

pail, which was favoured in Leeds and Halifax. According to the trade circular of the Goux Company, the bottom of these pails was covered with three or four inches of refuse which might consist of 'stable litter, leaves, spent tan or hops, sawdust, shavings, shoddy, flax dressings, or the thousand-and-one convenient substances to be found in every place.'

This was mixed with 'a little soot, charcoal, gypsum, or other deodorizer.' In order to line the sides of the pail, a solid mould was produced, round which a similar mixture was tightly packed. 'The preparation of the tub is not a lengthy process, and requires no special skill; one boy can pack a hundred tubs in an hour, and, when once ready for use, no other precaution has to be taken; nothing is needed but to remove the charged tub at stated times and replace it with a clean one.' In a testimonial statement, the then Medical Officer of Health for Leeds wrote that there had only been two complaints about Goux pails in the course of five years. Murphy, though he dealt fairly enough with the use of ashes, really went to town on earth closets: 'The effect of dry earth upon excreta is very different from that of ashes, for it is found that it serves to make the excreta not only inoffensive, but to effect complete change in the latter, so that their original character cannot be recognized, and even if paper be mixed with them this disappears at the same time.'

Two conditions were essential: the earth had to be very dry and very finely sifted. It could be dried over the kitchen fire or on the hearth under a kitchen range or in the sun—an extra chore which the modern householder is happily spared—in which case it was recommended that enough earth was dried in the summer to last through the winter. The ingenuity of the eighteen-eighties also offered the labour-saving device of a special stove for earth drying, shaped like a table with a tray on top and a small furnace beneath. Patent sifters were also on sale. The application of the earth, moreover, was a matter of choice. It could be done 'by a mere scoop in the hand of the user, or by a mechanical contrivance in connection with the closet; the latter method is the better, for it eliminates any chance of improper application through the carelessness of the individual.'

Moule's Earth-Closet Company used an ingenious device, patented in 1860 by the Rev. Henry Moule, in which the earth could be discharged either by a plug or by pressure on the seat.

Finally there was charcoal, much used among shipbuilding communities of the Clyde: 'Mr. Edward Stanford, who has especially urged the value of this material for closet use, has found by experiment that, whereas dry clay only absorbs 45 per cent of water, dry charcoal prepared from seaweed absorbs 147 per cent. The closet to be used is practically the same as the earth-closet, but for the charcoal system it is claimed that chamber urine may be thrown on to it in addition to that which accompanies each dejection. After removal, the mixture is burnt in a retort, which distils over products which are said to have a value of a material kind, while the residue is used over again.'

A hundred years ago there were still cesspools in London's Red Lion Square and Bedford Row. For centuries the contents of cesspits of urban houses were simply carted away, sometimes where the smallest room happened to be inconveniently sited having to be carried through from the back of the house to the front. Not till 1863 did London achieve a system of main drainage or sewers. No wonder Wilkie Collins moving into his house in Gloucester Place two years later wrote to his mother with such glee: 'A certain necessary place has got the most lovely new pan you ever saw. It's quite a pleasure to look into it.'

Though the installation of a water closet in the New England home of Henry Wadsworth Longfellow as early as 1840 is said to have aroused the widest local interest in such new-fangled devices, the recollections of Carl Sandburg, many years later as an enlisted man in the Illinois Volunteers after the outbreak of the Spanish War of 1898, suggest that the New World was not in every respect ahead of Victorian London. 'For the ritual relief of bowels or bladder we walked some two hundred yards to the "vaults." These were dug about six feet deep and three feet wide. At the sides were poles cut from the near-by woods and laid on crotched sticks with no overhead cover from the midday sun or a midnight rain. I saw no lime or sand thrown over the deposits to reduce the stench or the swarming flies. This likewise was seven miles from the City of Washington where the Department of War had its office. . . . There were fellows who said they wished the stench could be wafted to the halls of Congress and the office of the Department of War seven miles away.'

And what of the army of emptiers that march so furtively through human history? They have not gone unrecorded. Sandburg himself as a boy of eleven or so had known and respected one such: 'About once a year a Negro we called Mister Elsey would come in the night with his wagon and clean the vault of our privy. He lived on Pine Street in a house he owned. We had respect for him and called him Mister. His work was always done at night. He came and went like a shadow in the moon.'

In Australia, as in many other parts of the English-speaking world, the name for them was, and perhaps still is, *nightmen*, and they were duly celebrated by a special ditty beginning:

> My father, he is but a nightman,
> He works up late hours at night . . .

The nightman's occupation is not necessarily confined to the hours of darkness. An uncle by marriage used to tell me as a child how in a Cornish township where he was brought up, the man with the cart would go round crying—with what now seems a fairly blunt disregard of the equality of the sexes—'Women! Women! Bring out your dungses!'

The sturdy Augean heroes of medieval England were usually called *gong fermors* (of which the records provide a diversity of spelling). *Gong* means simply a latrine or privy; and the rest of it derives from the verb to *fey*, or cleanse. Sometimes in our records they are mentioned by name. An item at Westminster in 1532 refers to 'Philip Longe, gongfermer, for the clensyng of certeyn jakis . . .'

Happily there is ample evidence that these heroic fellows received the rate for the job. Thirteen workmen employed for five days in cleaning the cesspit of Newgate Prison in 1262 received sixpence a day, which was about three times as much as the pay for unskilled workers at that time. The churchwardens of St. Mary-at-Hill in 1478 paid five shillings and fourpence for the voiding of a privy in a house belonging to the parish. But the *gong fermors* working by night were not always trusted to carry out their strenuous tasks without some supervision.

The Westminster records in 1536 show an item of eightpence paid to a man 'yat watched ye gong-farmers' for two nights.

A merry England! Perhaps. Yet its cities and towns must have stunk to high heaven, for not many of them were small enough to obey the precepts of Deuteronomy:

'Thou shalt have a place also without the camp, whither thou shalt go forth abroad:

'And thou shalt have a paddle upon thy weapon; and it shall be, when thou wilt ease thyself abroad, thou shalt dig therewith, and shalt turn back and cover that which cometh from thee:

'For the Lord thy God walketh in the midst of thy camp, to deliver thee, and to give up thine enemies before thee; therefore shall thy camp be holy: that He see no unclean thing in thee, and turn away from thee.'

The observance of these sensible laws, laid down for the nomadic tribes of Israel when smallest rooms were for the most part unthought of, would have saved mankind from many a plague even if the *gong fermors* had been kept out of business.

Such tribal peoples, and indeed many honest, decent, un-nomadic Europeans, to this very day, prefer what may be delicately contrasted as *squatting* to *perching*—a habit which fascinated but dismayed Mr. Fleet when he was constrained, in his younger days, to travel far and wide in the service of his country. He is not alone, I fancy, in recalling the moments of panic when one, unaccustomed but in great need, is directed to a smallest room innocent of any pedestal but equipped with outsize footprints for the squatter's comfort and a cavity beneath. Such equipment has had a modest place for years and still appears in the catalogues of manufacturers conscious of their duty and indeed of the commercial desirability to serve the needs of all mankind. The geographically vague but spacious adjective *Oriental* seems to be a favoured description among the specialists who cater for this particular need.

That they are wise in continuing to meet a demand so closely allied to habit was brought home to me by a Roumanian emigrant now well connected to the mains in the United States. In spite of his own adaptability, he held that a man is a creature of habit, more especially in the smallest room. His own uncle, an innkeeper, he added, to illustrate his point, installed the very first pedestal water closet in Valna. This was not only novel but luxurious, for it had a plush seat. The customers, alas, refused to allow the habits of a lifetime to be broken by such a luxurious innovation and were forever climbing up to stand upon the plush. 'Then my uncle—a man, you understand, of some initiative—placed a board overhead to ensure sitting. But what happened? People still climbed up and stood, crouching—but really crouching.'

There is an element of progressive snobbery, somewhat vigorously supported by Mr. Fleet, as well as by the nephew of the innkeeper of Valna, suggesting that the simple but practical arrangements of the squatter are not wholly civilized. After they occupied Belgium in the nineteen-forties, the Germans raised a sardonic monument to this theory near Ghent, on the road to St. Denijs Westrem and Courtrai. Their device, intended perhaps to intimidate, certainly to insult, their temporary subjects, was two up-ended 'Oriental types' complete with imprints and orifices, mounted upon a wall with a headstone between bearing the inscription, roughly translated from Flemish, 'In memory of the good old days before the barbarian Germans came.' I have a photograph, taken in 1944, of this fine piece of Nazi *Kultur* before me as I write. I cannot believe that it still exists.

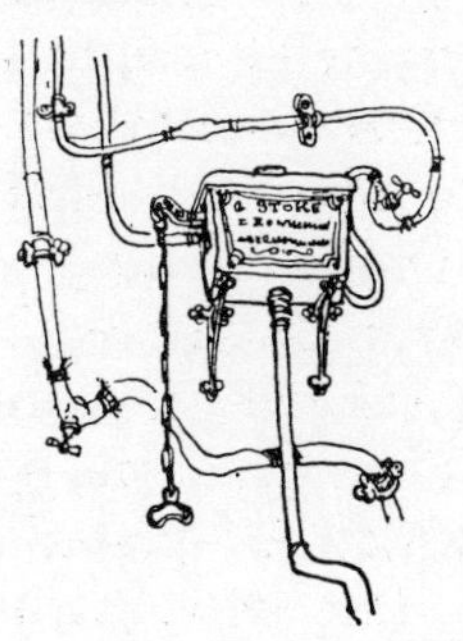

The Specialist

READING IN THE SMALLEST ROOM—MR. FLEET INTRODUCED TO LEM PUTT—'THE SPECIALIST' AND ITS AUTHOR CHIC SALE—G. B. S. AND ITS FIRST PUBLICATION IN ENGLAND—OTHER SPECIALIZED WORKS

'I KNEW a gentleman,' wrote Lord Chesterfield to his son in 1747, 'who was so good a manager of his time, that he would not even lose that small portion of it, which the call of nature obliged him to pass in the necessary-house; but gradually went through all the Latin poets, in those moments. He bought, for example, a common edition of Horace, of which he tore off gradually a couple of pages, carried them with him to that necessary place, read them first, and then sent them down as a sacrifice to Cloacina: thus was so much time fairly gained; and I recommend you to follow his example. It is better than only doing what you cannot help doing at those moments; and it will make any book which you shall read in that manner, very present to your mind.'

Though Mr. Fleet is a traditionalist in so many other respects, in matters of hygiene and democracy he is obstinately *avant-garde*. A casual reference to the calling in of George the carpenter to construct a bookshelf in our smallest room filled Mr. Fleet with dismay. 'Looks like you're letting this little old place go to your head,' he said, his lips pursed up with disapproval.

I recall the more expansive moments of Mr. Fleet when, over a pint, he chose to rail at Fred the mason over the size of the window at first proposed for our smallest room. 'Trouble with you masons is you're so set on your stonework, you can't even leave space to let the light in,' he had said.

'Windows is draughty,' Fred the mason had countered, defending his craft.

'You take no account of hygiene, I suppose? Don't fresh air and ventilation mean nothing to you, Fred?'

'Pain in the neck, most likely.'

'Then you ought to shut the window when you're in there.'

'Smaller the window, less you have to shut out, Mr. Fleet.'

'Mean to tell me that a man with your know-how wouldn't put in a window big enough to let anybody read his Sunday paper?'

'Sporting results and all?' said Fred, attempting to throw off this unexpected attack with a laugh. 'Depends on his eyesight, that do.'

'Sporting results and all! A man's entitled to read all through on a Sunday if he's a mind to,' Mr. Fleet had thundered his last word; and it was with this in mind that I meekly suggested to him that the provision of a bookshelf in the smallest room could contribute at once to mental hygiene and to spiritual uplift. 'After all, there's no reason why the scheme of things should be limited to a Sunday newspaper,' I said, recalling the mail-order catalogue of Lem Putt.

'Depends how many's knocking at the door!' Mr. Fleet asserted his democratic note. 'Them as has *two* can afford to be highfalutin' and read Shakespeare . . . but books in general isn't hygienic,' he added, switching to the other tack.

'You don't mean that George should make us a plastic bookshelf?'

'Not till there's people like yourself in the book trade who'll catch up with the times and give us plastic books.'

'That may come,' I made a last dispirited attempt to quell Mr. Fleet. 'But not until such sportsmen as yourself read your results in plastic newspapers.'

Mr. Fleet hesitated. He denied me my triumph. I guessed that he shared with Lord Chesterfield's 'good manager of his time,' a secondary use of the reading material he carried to the smallest room. 'This is a free world,' he said, 'and any man is entitled to read a newspaper on a Sunday morning wherever he chooses. But books . . .'

Mr. Fleet had never become acquainted with *The Specialist*, and my real triumph, to celebrate the completion of our smallest room, was to present him with a copy.

'I'm not a great one on books,' said he at first, with his usual talent for emphasizing the obvious.

Later he said, 'That one's kept me abed a good bit of Sunday morning, reading and reading again. And after I'd done with it, I lay wondering whether or not I ought to show it to the missus.'

He permitted himself a knowing grin. 'It don't do to leave such a book about.'

'Doesn't shock a practical man like you, surely?'

'Trouble is how I'm going to keep it safe and sound without it being lifted.'

I explained that we proposed to chain a copy of *The Specialist* in our smallest room, just as better men in better times chained a better book for better reasons in Chipperley Church.[1] Mr. Fleet forgot his disapproval of our bookshelf in seeing this as a rare joke. 'I reckon you're not the first that's chained him up, nor the last, neither.'

Then he added his grudging but heartfelt tribute to the little masterpiece of Chic Sale. 'You'd have to travel a bit to find a book like that. And it ain't too long either.'

The Specialist is only about three thousand words long. Translations of it have appeared in ten languages. In the United States alone the sales had

[1] Even better men, judging by Wilson Harris's reminiscences of a Quaker upbringing in *Life So Far*, have ensured that God's time is not wasted, by hanging a Holy Bible from a bracket in the lavatory.

passed the million mark by the time the book reached its twenty-fifth anniversary—and of course the polite euphemism a *Chic Sale* has become a part of the American slanguage. Charles Sale, known to his friends as Charlie and to the world as Chic, was a dentist's son born at Huron in the old Dakota Territory in 1884. He died in 1936 with an international reputation as the author of what must be the shortest best-seller the world has ever known.

During Chic's boyhood in the 'nineties his father moved his dental surgery to Urbana, Illinois, and it was there that Chic found his copy in the person of a home-town carpenter whose one characteristic—according to Mrs. Chic Sale, who happened to visit me in London while I was writing these words—was a splendid walrus moustache. This original hirsute Specialist, Lem Putt, speaking the Hoosier dialect beloved of Mark Twain, left upon young Charlie Sale a lasting impression of that homely basic humour, which first broke upon the world in print some three decades later in 1929, and which still delights people of discrimination and goodwill nearly two decades after the author's death.

Nevertheless it was almost by chance, and almost reluctantly, that Chic Sale became a writer. He set out with no such intention. He chose the boards as his career; and it was as a vaudeville artist that this son of the Middle West built up a States-wide reputation. Touring America as a 'headliner' in vaudeville, Chic became also a popular turn at those luncheons which are such an integral and characteristic part of the American way of life. It was good

AN ILLUSTRATION BY WILLIAM KERMODE
FOR THE ENGLISH EDITION OF 'THE SPECIALIST'

publicity for his vaudeville show to make after-lunch appearances at the functions of such fraternities as the Lion Club, the Kiwanians, the Elks, and the Rotarians. He was shy about public speaking unless it was to put over an act in character. So he began to tell stories about Lem Putt. He was a true pro., studying his audience. Thoughts of being a best-selling writer never crossed his mind. He just worked hard to stay at the top of his profession. His friend Charles Walton, recalling him, sends me this memory. 'Chic was one of the greatest actors that the American stage produced, and the secret of that I think lies in a story about an MGM sales convention in Kansas City. . . . He found what he thought was a common ground, which was that there are two kinds of actors and two kinds of salesmen. . . . He illustrated the point by saying that the man who goes out with an order book, says to the customer "What do you want?" and writes it down, is just a salesman. Similarly, the actor who learns the words, puts on his costume and make-up and recites the words as dramatically as he can, is just an actor. However, the salesman who believes in his product and goes out and meets a prospect, who doesn't want to buy his product, nevertheless is so imbued with the value of that product that by real salesmanship he finally convinces the man and gets the order. That is a real salesman. Likewise, the actor who learns his part, puts on his costume and his make-up and then *makes up inside*. . . . He is a real actor. . . .

'Then, to illustrate this point, standing there in tuxedo Chic Sale, as himself, recited James Whitcomb Riley's poem, "S'long Jim, take ker yourself." It is a poem about a father who is saying good-bye to his son who is going into the war, he has a million things to say, but the only thing he can think of is, "S'long Jim, take ker yourself." When Chic finished, there was wild applause. When he had calmed them down, he said "That's just acting," then he told me that he put a hump in his back, screwed up his face, made his hands look old and gnarled, put a quaver in his voice, and in the high pitch of an aged man recited the same poem. Then pandemonium broke loose. Chic stole the show.'

When he was telling his Lem Putt anecdotes, Chic, according to Mrs. Sale, would assist this 'inside make-up' of his with only one prop. He would sometimes draw out of his pocket a walrus moustache, the likeness of that worn by the home-town carpenter back in Urbana in the 'nineties.

The fame of the Lem Putt act brought with it the danger of plagiarism and a risk that the material might be pirated in print. Two newspapermen in St. Louis persuaded Chic to take action to protect his copyright. With their help, he made plans to write and print the essential Lem Putt, the Specialist 'sincere in his work as a good painter whose heart is in his canvas.' Needless to say, he ran right up against literary *taboo.* American publishers who were ready to laugh after luncheon declared themselves to be sympathetic and interested when they encountered *The Specialist* in the austerity of their own offices, but could not screw up enough courage to print it. Nobody seems to know quite how many allowed the midget best-seller to slip through their hands. Enough, at least, to allow Chic Sale to be persuaded by the two St. Louis newspapermen that the only course was to start a publishing firm and print it themselves. Thus the Specialist Publishing Company was founded and Charles Walton recalls how the author went about his task of rigorous selection:

'So, after Chic decided to print *The Specialist*, he would take each of the incidents of Lem Putt's experiences and he would try them out on an audience, then as he recited each one, he would note the audience reaction, whether it fell flat or whether he got a belly laugh. Then, if a point didn't go over to his satisfaction, he would work it over and try it out on the next audience; so, when it came to publishing *The Specialist* he selected those that his experience before audiences had proven to be sure-fire and these were collected for *The Specialist*.'

The two St. Louis newspapermen found they had a full-time assignment on their hands and threw up their jobs. In a matter of months, the Specialist Publishing Company had to move its offices three times to cope with the orders that poured in from all over America. The little thirty-page book achieved a fame which almost panicked its sponsors. Correspondence and criticism, as well as orders, poured in. Chic Sale, ever sensitive to audience reaction, was for the rest of his life warmed and tirelessly attentive to the thousands of correspondents who sent him well-meant but quite useless material ranging from single anecdotes to complete life stories. Marie Sale, his widow, remembers, too, how sickened he was, not only by the criticism and denunciation which came from the strait-laced, but also by the spate of vulgar and even pornographic correspondence that reached him.

By the end of 1929, the fame of his slender saga of American country life had already crossed the Atlantic. In England, a prince of the royal blood, with the harmless intention of entertaining his intimate friends, pirated an edition by producing a dozen typewritten copies. Then a gift copy was sent by a New York bookseller to the chairman of the publishing house of Putnams in London.

Putnams had already encountered the strength of the literary *taboos* of the period by publishing such works as Erich Maria Remarque's *All Quiet on the Western Front*. Putnams—and I must here declare my interest and mention that I am a director of this publishing house, though what happened was long before my time—were enchanted by *The Specialist* and encouraged by the news that it was selling, over the counter, not under the counter, in New York, like hot cakes. Could the literary *taboos* be defied? In January, 1930, they wrote to George Bernard Shaw: 'May we consult you about a small, and, to our mind, innocently Rabelaisian little American book which we have undertaken to publish in England? . . .

'By the nature of the subject probably a certain number of readers will shun it as obscene while others will pore over it for the same reason. We should like to suggest to the public that there is no need to be excited, but that there is harmless amusement in the book for people of honest mind and a sense of humour. If you agree with us, would you consider contributing a brief Introduction?'

Shaw sent one of his famous printed postcards, which his thousands of literary correspondents will recall, ending with the words: 'A request for a preface by him is therefore a request for a gift of some months of hard professional work. When this is appreciated it will be seen that even with the best disposition towards his correspondents it is not possible for Mr. Shaw to oblige them in this particular manner.'

This was followed by a spidery scrawl of appreciation and encouragement: 'Besides, pioneering masterpieces like Mr. Sale's must stand on their own legs. I have quite enough to answer for in my own works without taking other authors on my shoulders as well. The illustrations are excellent; but the frontispiece fails in courage. Clearly it should represent the Elmer family *in situ*. G. B. S.'

This last comment did not refer to the now famous illustrations by William Kermode, whose name, contrary to general belief, is not a *nom de guerre*. Mr. Kermode tells me that he happened to hear, through the printers, that new illustrations were proposed. He hastened at once to the publishers and said: 'Obviously with my name I demand to do them.'

Putnams replied to Shaw that they feared the public might regard the book as contraband unless told by someone of influence that it was really all right, adding that, as publishers, they had felt a bit uneasy until they had received this measure of encouragement. They went on, by way of thanks, to offer the great man several copies of the book on publication for him to give away. Characteristically G. B. S. wrote: 'I never give away books. If I gained a reputation for such a wicked practice my life would not be worth anything. And how is Mr. Sale to live if his books are to be had for nothing?

'I forgot to say that as far as I recollect the definition of obscenity by L. C. J. Cockburn, which is the one relied on in *The Well of Loneliness* case, *The Specialist* is not obscene; and any new definition that would include it would also make the works of Smollett liable to prosecution. This does not come to much, as the Cockburn definition makes not only the Bible but every possible work of romantic fiction liable; but you may note it for what it is worth. G. Bernard Shaw.'

Though *The Specialist* has never been out of print from that day to this, and paradoxically had a suddenly increased sale here when American servicemen came to England during the Second World War, literary advice at the outset was divided. Sir Desmond MacCarthy's, for instance, did not agree with that of G. B. S. 'I think *The Specialist* is rather disappointing, and I don't believe that it will amuse the frivolous elect enough, while the jolly, coarse, crude public hardly exists at all in England, but of course I may be wrong.'

How many of us, I wonder, would have agreed with that eminent critic at the time. That he proved to be wrong is not perhaps to his discredit so much as to the credit of that much maligned creature 'the average reader,' who has proved over the years that prudery in these matters is a form of faint-hearted oppression which might be funny were it not all too often so viciously applied.

Chic Sale inspired others, good and bad. Greeting-cards in which privies and water closets are depicted as accessories to slapstick situations and coarse ribaldry still emanate from the west coast of America. At least one of these, carrying a poem called

'The Passing of the Backhouse,' by James Whitcomb Riley (the Hoosier poet Chic loved to quote), portrays a Lem Putt structure and carries a birthday greeting 'From one Specialist to another.' Such cards, I am assured, are no mere blague but a social comment. 'They come not from under any counter, but from the centre of Los Angeles's famed Farmer's Market, where a bright, very *bien élevée* little old lady sells them to typical beaming tourists of all ages, not very often at all seasoned scatologists.'

A small volume called *The Amateur* declaring itself to be an answer to *The Specialist* is printed in Toronto, but has the Bush of Australia as its setting and introduces the word *Dub*, which is a novelty to many of us. 'I might tell you Privy's a new name to us out here, bein' as we was all brought up to call it the Dub, and me eight children after me, and the Littley when they was tiny mites . . .' states the elderly female narrator of this vigorous little work.

There is a certain amount of information mingled with archness and heavy humour in another little anonymous work called *Old English Easances*, published with characteristic pseudonymic humour by Sitwell and Wayte Ltd., a joke-book which is hardly worthy of the shelf that George built in our smallest room. *Cleanliness and Godliness*, by Reginald Reynolds, published by Allen and Unwin in 1945, is a scholarly, robustly controversial book of great interest and importance in spite of its many lapses into stylistic pedantry.

Professor D. W. Brogan has described the complaint of an American that there are 'not enough toilets in Britain' as being the height of impudence. 'I doubt if there are a hundred public toilets in the U.S.,' the savant went on, 'and I think I have been in all of them.' This claim reminds me of another scholar claiming comprehensive knowledge in these matters, one describing himself as Paul Pry upon the title page of a useful little work called *For Your Convenience*, published by Routledge in 1937. This sets out, in the form of a 'learned dialogue instructive to all Londoners and London visitors' an account of the public conveniences (stressing the value of museums to those in need) available at that time, the endpapers of the book offering pictorial maps showing where these, fifty-one in number, were (and are, in spite of Hitler's undiscriminating bombs, mostly still) situated. It is a book which will undoubtedly ease the rustic anxiety of Mr. Fleet when I lend it to him for the London visit he undertakes, once every five years or so, to see some exhibition of contemporary sanitary equipment, thus keeping abreast and seeing the sights—but always, he admits, with a persistent dread of being taken short.

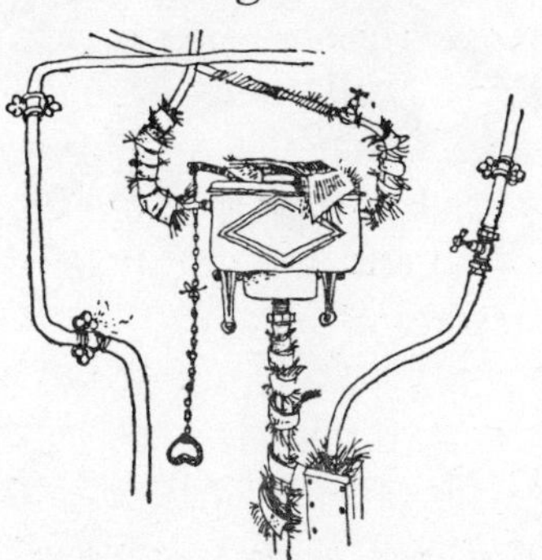

RAILWAYS

Mobility and Utility

THE AIRBORNE PRIVY—ITS BEGINNINGS—ITS TECHNICAL PROBLEMS—EARLY RAILWAY CLOSETS—MOBILE AND TEMPORARY CONVENIENCES—COALMINES—CORONATIONS—INHIBITED FISHERMEN

'IN ships at sea, there's *the heads*, and the poor devil that gets the task of doing 'em is always the *captin of the heads*,' Mr. Fleet reminisced, surveying the progress of our smallest room one day as a formation of jet aircraft snored overhead. 'What puzzles me about them as chooses to risk their necks up aloft there is how do they *manage*. . . ?'

George the carpenter, who had served in the Air Force during the Second World War, explained briefly about the cans that were handed round to meet the needs of those who flew in the less-long range aircraft that did not qualify for a metal, built-in Jericho.

'But,' said George, in his knowing way, 'there's proper closets everywhere now—every bit as good as in trains or ships.'

'That must be quite an experience . . . that must,' Mr. Fleet observed, I thought a little wistfully, as he contemplated, perhaps for the first time, the idea of an airborne privy. 'Must take a lot of nerve though to sit there while you're flying through the air.'

A smallest room clearly had no place in the austerely practical economy of military aircraft design —except where the fulfilment of an aviator's need offered a positive tactical advantage. There is no record of any airborne comfort until after the First World War. The world's first regular passenger air service between London and Paris and Amsterdam in 1919–20, did not pander in any way to the needs of their excited and nervous customers. By 1922, however, the need had been met, and handsomely, aboard the De Havilland DH-34 aircraft put into service by both the Instone Air Line and the Daimler Airway running scheduled services between Britain and the Continent. The Dutch Fokker planes, which came into service from 1924 onwards, were fitted with open affairs, borrowed in kind, perhaps, from the nineteenth-century railways. These have been described as 'a hole in the floor through which the draught had a tendency to enter with some force.' The aeronaut who offers this information adds that it explains why it was possible from time to time to find golden sovereigns, gent's pipes, and ladies' lockets in the streets of London. When in October, 1927, Juan Trippe started Pan-American Airways with a contract to carry mail between America and Cuba and a small fleet of Fokker F-7 aeroplanes, he was making aviation history, though I can find no evidence that the closets which were such a vaunted feature of his aircraft were actually the first airborne conveniences in the United States. Cy Caldwell describes Tony Fokker's masterpieces as containing '. . . a toilet with a built-in updraft—which he discovered to his surprise

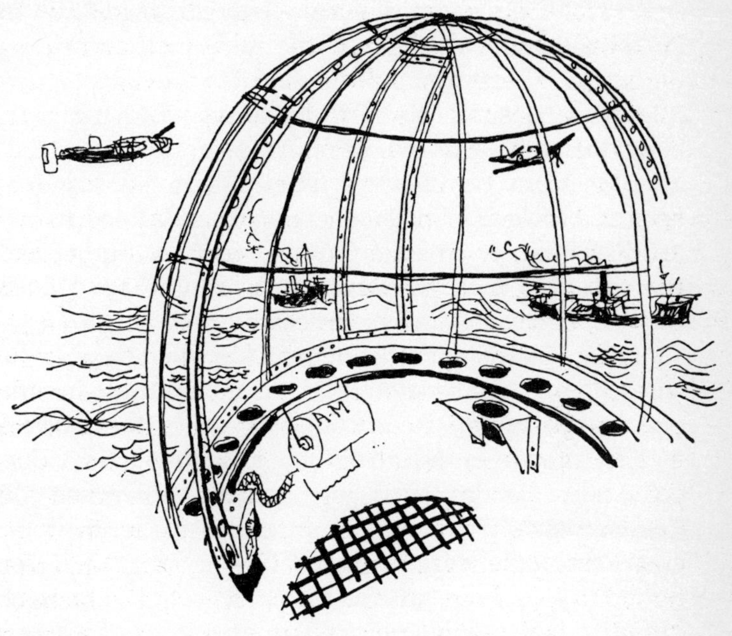

when he gave it a test, personally, during a trial flight.'

Those with long memories of air travel agree that there has been nothing scenically to equal the views obtained during transatlantic flights from the tail turrets of Liberators which, toward the end of the Second World War, were converted into smallest rooms. Here, surrounded by transparency, the sitter enjoyed a panorama from a vantage point, according to aeronautical savants, unequalled in aviation history. Nevertheless, visits there had to be brief. My own recollection is that these were quite the coldest smallest rooms ever devised. Indeed, a metal rod was kept handy to chip off the ice which formed at the base of the throne.

It may be some comfort to those who, like Mr. Fleet, distrust the whole business, to know that there is now no danger from falling sovereigns, pipes, or lockets. Air Navigation Regulations forbid the discharge of sewage from aircraft in flight, and that includes such by-products as might have been considered treasure trove in less hygienic days.

It may be of some comfort, too, for those who believe that civilization can be measured in the terms of hygiene, to know that while the Second World War was still raging, a Ministerial Committee in London was sitting in conference on chemical closets and their future uses in aircraft. Their recommendations were far-reaching, and for the most part too abstruse for these pages. Let it be said only that manufacturers and operators of aircraft have always been constrained to treat the appearance, size, number and, above all, weight of their airborne smallest rooms with the utmost seriousness. An airline operator of my acquaintance, for instance, confided the fact that his concern, unable naturally enough to carry the necessary staff to find out how frequently passengers were in need during flights, had fitted a mechanical device to the doors of their airborne closets, a sort of secret ray that recorded the frequency of use on various flights. In spite of this scientific research, there was subsequent miscalculation over the closet space required. To the dismay of all—and there is nothing airline operators apparently so much dread—queues of anxious passengers formed in some post-war airliners.

Since then progress has been made. It is now stated by the pundits that the number of passengers per closet which can be accepted for first-class air travel is twenty-four. For second-class the figure is given as thirty, so it seems that a measure of continence is necessary for those of us who desire to fly on the cheap. Aboard the larger aircraft, polite discrimination is afforded between male and female passengers: but even this nicety is not without its technical problems, for statistics show that there is an overall preponderance of masculine air passengers, thus causing, according to the painstaking individuals who have to worry about these things, 'uneven loading of the closet containers.'

Most considerate touch of all—and one which was not lost on us when we found ourselves in conference with Mr. Fleet, Fred, and George about the colour-scheme suggested by Percy the painter for our own smallest room—is the care lavished by the airliner people upon closet decoration.

Because sharp contrasts of colour are thought to be a cause of air-sickness, a first requirement is that the decoration of an airborne smallest room shall blend with that of the passenger cabins. Certain colours are condemned as affecting the 'emotional tone' of passengers,[1] 'the effect depending primarily on conditioned associations from their past experience.' Yellow is said to accentuate nausea. The lighter shades

[1] G. S. Bowey, A.M.I.Mech.E., A.F.R.Ae.S., writing in *Aircraft Engineering*.

of grey are hailed as 'colours to be used as calming influences in the psychological reactions of passengers.'

Railroad passengers have rarely, if ever, been cosseted to this extent. The very first first-class passengers who had their own coaches hoisted on to railway-bogeys were able to resort to the useful and often ornate pots that were kept under their well-upholstered seats for emergencies. These vessels could be rich and fanciful in design. When as a youth I was employed as a rent-collector in London, I had on my roll a silversmith, one of the proud surviving craftsmen of Soho, who in his youth had specialized in the fashioning of carriage pots of silver, wonderfully decorated with fancies and with the armorial bearings of European royalty and nobility. He would recall them and describe them in moments of rhetorical nostalgia when he was behind with his rent. At such times, and they were frequent enough, he would assert that in the world of armorial art the word *overdue* was commonplace and indeed to be despised.

Since then I have learnt on the authority of a mid-Victorian expert on fiscal matters, D. M. Evans, that our ancient nobility did not stop at silver. Evans mentions a firm of eminent bankers who about the middle of the seventeenth century advanced the then substantial sum of fifteen pounds to a Scottish lady of title on the security of her gold *pot-de-chambre*. He omits her title but goes on to say that it was still in existence when he was writing in 1856, and there is the possibility therefore that by that time the pot itself, if the family ever got it back, may have already travelled beneath the seat of a family coach on railway-bogeys.

For the ordinary run of early railroad passengers, there were no arrangements whatever; and patience was the only necessity. At early morning stops, men were wont to salute the sunrise, as decorously as they might, at the ends of platforms, while women stood in earnest conversation here and there, their long skirts providing cover even though the platform itself offered little by way of camouflage.

The credit for alleviating this distress among long-distance rail passengers goes to America, where as early as the 'fifties, according to Mr. C. Hamilton Ellis, that omniscient exponent of railroad lore and procedure, the railroad cars were provided each with a small compartment fitted with a bottomless jakes. In the 'sixties, central European carriages bore a notice *Abort im Gepackwagen*, and for many years the Spaniards kept their necessaria in the guard's van.

England, it seemed, lagged behind in providing for the common man and his mate, though for Queen Victoria herself, provision was made as early as 1848. The meeting of her royal needs may well have been the active spur to inventiveness. The old South Eastern's royal saloon, built during 1850, sported two small sofas, one of which contained a 'patent convenience.' This again, which seems to have been a cross between a closet and a commode, was in use ten years later in an invalid carriage. It was not in fact till the 'sixties that British railway companies installed closets—and then only in saloon carriages for hire by parties. The first sleeping-car in Great Britain, which ran on the North British Railway in 1873, however, had a real closet; and the first Pullman cars to be imported from America, a year later, were fitted with valve water closets. The first ordinary side-corridor coach which appeared on the Great Northern in 1881 indulged in a luxury of segregation which has since disappeared, being fitted with a *Ladies* at one end and a *Gents* at the other. The 'eighties brought a triumph when, according to Hamilton Ellis, 'the Midland Railway built a composite compartment-type carriage with lavatories for both first and third class. It was sent to the Paris Exhibition of 1881, and the French were so excited, not only by its beautiful workmanship but at its provision of both soft seats and *chaises percées* for the commonalty, that they awarded it the *Grand Prix*.'

Yet it was Paris in the days of the Empire that witnessed what must have been one of the earliest of all travelling closets. It is said that Singer of sewing-machine fame, one of whose quirks was to dress from head to foot in red, would accomplish the fashionable drive round the lake in the Bois in an immense vehicle with a dressing-room and a lavatory at the back.

Mobility in closets is not indeed a quality which is entirely without precedent. Pigot and Co.'s Commercial Directory of London for 1826–27 carried an advertisement by S. Hawkins of 167 Fleet Street, for a newly-invented self-acting *portable* water closet holding royal letters patent.

In the hurry-scurry of our own age, the portable

closet, managed not by water but by chemistry, has come into its own not only aloft but down below. In many of those British coalmines, where, at the time when Hawkins of Fleet Street was advertising his sybaritic convenience for the leisured, women and children were toiling like driven animals, there are now portable chemical conveniences for the workers at the coalface. These underground smallest rooms are fitted with transporter tanks which run on pit railways, thus enabling those who delve to share the amenities of those who fly.

The praiseworthy modern conception of a convenience being not just static but alert, as it were, to human need, owes something to the almost outmoded piston engine. In the years when swords were being beaten into ploughshares, Air Force trailers were converted into eight-seater closets with appurtenances for use at race meetings and such other open-air events where the British lady, penny in hand, finds herself in a quandary while the British gent sneaks behind canvas or takes to the woods.

Some enterprising seaside municipalities have refitted their obsolete buses with chemical, in place of fare-paying, seats in order to serve outlying beaches upon which visitors are thick on the sand and which are not, as the Australians would say, sewered.

Of the transient here-today-and-gone-tomorrow smallest rooms with which modern science now meets human need, few could enjoy more adventitious glamour than those installed for a British coronation. All the world knows that one of the more impressive aspects of the ceremonial religious crowning of a monarch at Westminster is the time it takes. All the world wonders *how people manage*. Now I was one of the seven-thousand-odd carefully dressed and thoughtfully equipped (as to food and drink) guests commanded to attend the Abbey for the coronation of Queen Elizabeth II. Afterwards, the most persistent questions from the under-privileged, who saw so much more of the event than I did by staying at home and watching television, concerned the arrangements made to answer the calls of Nature, it being common knowledge that many of us were summoned at 6.30 a.m. and not released until early afternoon. I first encountered these arrangements when I was privileged to attend a dress rehearsal of the ceremony and, fighting back *folie de grandeur*, was assigned to the crimson chair to be occupied on the great day by a duchess. It was, in short, one of the best positions; but the illusion of scarlet and ermine did not entirely assuage human frailty—or curiosity. Upon my making known my need, I was ushered into the twilight by superbly clad officials with all the indulgent concern flaunted upon a spoilt child. When at length I found it, this smallest room, I realized that I had travelled east to the very steps of the altar. There, made fast by the frailest of bolts, concealed by the tenderest of prefabricated walls, to a majestic surge of ceremonial music, I usurped a throne. There were two hundred and thirteen chemical closets in Westminster Abbey on that day, forming a veritable rally of smallest rooms within those stately walls. Before a former coronation, an exalted and notoriously practical royal lady had inspected one of such conveniences and pointed out, perhaps from memory of sad experience, a serious defect. The little thrones were right up against the wall, as they might be in any conventional smallest room. But how could a Personage encompassed with splendid layers of ceremonial clothing *manage*?

The people who equipped the Abbey, and incidentally look after many of the coalmines, say that 'no extra special Models (their word for them) were requested although on other royal functions a special type, fitted with arm rests, had been used.' Those in the Triforium, to which I was privileged to be banished for the event itself, were a solace to us all, more particularly to the Far-Eastern newspaper reporter who, during the Creed, resorted in the sanctity of a smallest room to a fragrant cheroot.

If too little has been made here of the problems and hazards of those who travel by water, it is, of course, because waterborne craft by their very nature are usually able to accommodate the human need. There have rarely been complaints about the facilities offered in larger vessels, though in smaller craft social problems have been known to arise. There are, too, unfortunate people such as John and Finlay Macphade who have been actually inhibited by a state of mobility. Their story is told by one Martin Martin, whose description of the Western Islands of Scotland at the turn of the seventeenth century was dedicated to Queen Anne's consort, Prince George of Denmark, whose smallest room we shall, in the next chapter, take the liberty of exploring. '. . . they lived on the coast, and went often a fishing, and after they had spent some nine or ten hours at sea, their bellies would swell; for after all their endeavours to get passage either way, it was impracticable until they came to land, and then they found no difficulty in the thing. This was a great inconvenience to any boat's crew in which either of these three men had been fishing, for it obliged them often to forbear when the fishing was most plentiful, and to row to the shore with any of these men that happened to become sick; for landing was the only remedy. At length one of their companions thought of an experiment to remove this inconvenience; he considered that when any of these men had got their feet on dry ground, they could then ease nature with as much freedom as any other person; and therefore he carried a large green turf of earth to the boat, and placed the green side uppermost, without telling the reason. One of these men who was subject to the infirmity above mentioned, perceiving an earthen turf in the boat, was surprised at the sight of it, and enquired for what purpose it had been brought thither? He that laid it there answered that he had done it to serve him, and that when he was disposed to ease nature he might find himself on land though he was at sea. The other took this as an affront, so that from words they came to blows; their fellows with much ado did separate them, and blamed him that brought the turf into the boat, since such a fancy could produce no other effect than a quarrel. All of them employed their time eagerly in fishing, until some hours after that the angry man, who before was so much affronted at the turf, was so ill of the swelling of his belly as usual, that he begged of the crew to row to the shore, but this was very disobliging to them all. He that intended to try the experiment with the turf, bid the sick man stand on it, and he might expect to have success by it; but he refused and still resented the affront which he thought was intended upon him; but at last all the boat's crew urged him to try what the turf might produce, since it could not make him worse than he was. The man being in great pain was by their repeated importunities prevailed upon to stand with his feet on the turf; and it had the wished effect, for nature became obedient both ways; and then the angry man changed his note, for he thanked his doctor whom he had some hours before beat. And from that time none of these three men ever went to sea without a green turf in their boat, which proved effectual. This is matter of fact, sufficiently known and attested by the better part of the parishioners still living upon the place.'

Could such a practical and discreet psychological device be of any assistance to those who have to study the needs of air travellers in this age?

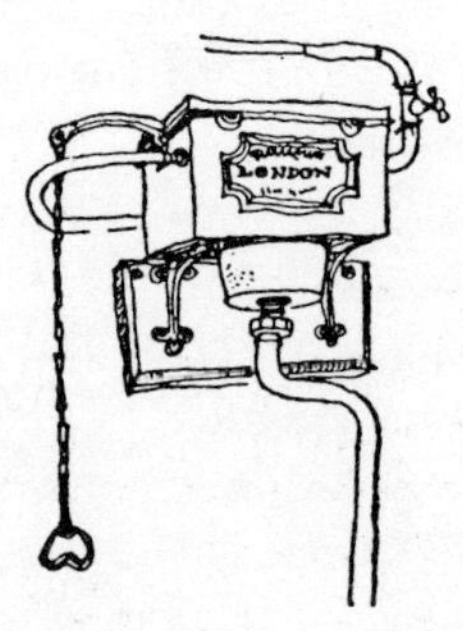

Catastrophe

CATASTROPHES IN THE SMALLEST ROOM—ON BEING LOCKED IN—A ROYAL DILEMMA—MR. FLEET'S PREDICAMENT—AN UNLOVED RELATIVE IMPRISONED—AN INCIDENT AT CHEQUERS—A NAUTICAL REVENGE—FATE OF A SCEPTIC—IMPERIAL CATASTROPHE—ORDEAL BY ANTS—CATASTROPHE CONTRIVED

THERE is nothing in our youth so alarming or in our maturity so humiliating or in its subsequent telling so riotously funny, as the common catastrophe of being locked in a smallest room. In moments of youthful gaiety or of adult hilarity when we are at our least inhibited, one of the ditties enthusiastically rendered by all English-speaking people is:

Oh dear, what can the
 matter be,
Three old ladies locked
 in the lavatory.
They were there from
 Monday till Saturday
Nobody knew they were
 there . . .

For reasons that I have never quite understood, a

boisterous appreciation of lavatory humour has always been said to be the perquisite of schoolboys, commercial travellers, and professionals of the vaudeville stage. Yet I have heard this ditty sung, with the happy witless relish it demands, by gentlemen, and even ladies, quite unconnected with these three categories. Moreover, I suspect that there are few indeed who have participated in the singing of these words who have not at some time in their childhood suffered the nightmare panic of being locked in, with the very real attendant dread that 'Nobody knew they were there.'

It is, as I say, the most simple of mishaps, its sometimes ignominious, sometimes bizarre, consequences sparing neither high nor low. In a certain outpost of the British Empire, for example, during a former reign, the most elaborate arrangements were made for the reception and comfort of a party of royal visitors. As is so often the case, the whole affair was being managed in accordance with a strictly arranged timetable. This, in the midst of all its well-ordered pomp and circumstance, allowed for a brief acknowledgment of human needs. There was consternation, therefore, when an indispensable royal personage, taking advantage of the brief opportunities and of the facilities afforded, failed to re-emerge. This gave way to dismay when it was realized that the personage was locked in. There was a hurried discussion. There was whispered advice. As anxiety mounted, there was much straining at the door of this smallest room so decisively reluctant to yield up its honoured guest. Precious minutes were lost, but the day was saved by the hasty procurement of a small native boy who, with the necessary equipment and instructions, was hoisted up and lowered through the top of the smallest room.

Very soon afterwards he emerged triumphantly, followed by the liberated and, according to eye-witnesses, splendidly unruffled personage from this never-to-be-forgotten dilemma, causing a delay which mystified the waiting thousands.

When a similar predicament happened to Mr. Fleet and Percy the painter in far less ceremonial circumstances during the latter stages of the decoration of our own smallest room, they carried it off with much less sense of *noblesse oblige.* Mr. Fleet had called to make sure about the ball valve. It was an excuse, we suspected, to indulge himself in what he loved to call 'the advice of a practical man.' This included denigration by faint praise of the work of less gifted craftsmen and of ourselves for the whole conception of the place.

Much of this high purpose was wasted owing to the fact that Percy alone was there to provide an audience. Only Percy, neat, sprightly, absorbed in brushwork and in revivalist gospel. 'Don't want to disturb you, Perce. I'm not one to come between a man and his work, whatever the tint of it. . . .' Mr. Fleet had begun, disapprovingly caressing the ball valve.

'So long as you don't come between a man and his Maker. . . .' Percy began to preach rhythmically as he painted—and it might well have been about then that he shot the bolt and painted it over.

The more fervently—and furtively, for his shame

choked him—Mr. Fleet swore, the more fervently Percy attempted his conversion. He accompanied his homily with the vigorous application of a turps-soaked rag to the coagulated bolt. Nevertheless, it was a sudden panic-stricken cry of 'Let me out of here before I suffocate with paint and religion,' that drew our attention to the plight of our progressive—and some whispered agnostic—plumber. Mr. Fleet blushed when we helped him out through the window. He muttered sheepishly about it being a good thing that Fred had left enough space for an emergency exit. Yet there was a lack of equanimity about him, a lack of poise. Percy, who muttered about a blow-lamp, came off no better. A sense of ignominy was shared between these two who had so little in common but fortuitous imprisonment. No good to tell them that they might be the first but they would certainly not be the last. Our smallest room, unusable as it was, had begun to assert itself. That one of the first victims of this assertion should be Mr. Fleet himself is one of those jests which in a rural community are never allowed to be forgotten.

By way of comfort to those like Mr. Fleet who are unable to see anything funny in such a predicament, particularly if they themselves happen to be its victim, I quoted the experience of a member of the family who is wealthy, pompous, and not much loved. 'It cost him a good deal of money, Mr. Fleet. It only cost you a certain amount of time and a great deal of unnecessary anxiety.'

The relative I have in mind laid out a very large sum (and, having no expectations, we can speak of it without spite or envy) on acquiring a sumptuous apartment to witness Queen Elizabeth's coronation procession. No comfort was lacking. He was able to sleep there the night before while less fortunate but somewhat happier fellow-creatures laid out newspapers on the damp pavements below and huddled sleeplessly singing comic songs in the rain to pass away the long hours of waiting. In the morning, while the crowds below him munched sandwiches and poured tea from flasks, he enjoyed a liberal breakfast of scrambled egg and kidney with a choice of coffee or champagne for his guests as they arrived early to join him. As flunkeys arranged cushions, carpets and gilt chairs by the windows, and, elsewhere in the apartment, television sets, serveries for champagne and collations of chicken, salmon and lobster mayonnaise, these guests gracefully mustered. They were, of course, handpicked. A smattering of actual friends, no relatives (for our dislike is mutual), and, for the most part, clients, customers, and people of good connection who would be useful during the forthcoming reign. He referred to the expenditure, in his modest way, as 'making sure I get a chance of greeting my sovereign,' though I suspect it was justified in more businesslike terms in certain of his accounts.

At any rate, he thought it was all fully justified as he stood there, champagne in hand, wondering whether it would be a gesture of loyalty to douse his cigar at the Queen's approach. With this thought in mind, seeing that all his guests were comfortably ensconced on the balconies, and his staff briefly, and indeed, humanely dismissed to see what they could from perches on the roof, he retired to the apartment's smallest room, a modest place lined with pink-veined marble and lit by a stained-glass window.

'I can guess what happened to him,' said Mr. Fleet, grinning for the first time since his own catastrophe. 'It's the rich what gets the pleasure, eh? But go on. . . .'

The cheering swelled, but the patent lock of that unfamiliar but sumptuous smallest room did not yield. The stained-glass window opened a few inches on to an area from which everyone had, of course, departed to see the procession. The cries of the prisoner and the beating of his plump, beringed hands upon the door were drowned in the majestic force of London as the Queen went by. The hand-picked guests, absorbed in the spectacle, gave little thought to their host, each, if he did, supposing him to be on some other of the three balconies upon which the party was accommodated. Nobody missed him even when the last of the procession had passed and he sat there, hot, hoarse, and exhausted, hearing for the first time snatches of the television commentary as the cheering died away.

The staff returned at last and, with sounds of suppressed laughter, mingled promises to fetch the porter who had the secret of the door. Everybody was drinking champagne again when the prisoner emerged. Everyone congratulated him upon his splendid arrangements. The members of the staff were quickly sworn to silence. The host joined his guests in declaring, not without a hollow feeling inside, that there had never been a spectacle like it.

I should never have heard of the true nature of

my relative's catastrophe had it not been for the fact that the porter had so often drunk the Queen's health by the time he was sworn to secrecy that he went away regarding the whole thing as a great joke and, having served at one time with me in the war, brought it out with relish at our next reunion.

Nevertheless, I hastened to point out to Mr. Fleet that there have been individuals who, though locked in, were still not entirely cut off from events. Many will recall the story of a Victorian household (and Miss Gwen Raverat in *Period Piece* recalls it being told by her uncle Leonard Darwin) of a lady locked in on a Sunday morning and of how her brother-in-law, a clergyman (sometimes described even as her husband), took up his position on a chair outside the door and read the morning service aloud to her from outside.

A much more savage example of Sabbatarianism is mentioned in John Stow's *A Survey of London* of 1603: '. . . a Iewe at Tewkesbury fell into a Priuie on the Saturday and would not that day bee taken out for reuerence of his sabbath, wherefore Richard Clare Earle of Glocester kepte him there till Munday that he was dead . . .'

Amid the spate of reminiscence offered by the political and military leaders of the Second World War, it was inevitable that there should be an anecdote about being locked in. General H. H. Arnold of the United States Air Force, introducing the popular American euphemism *johnny*, describes an incident at Chequers. He had dined there with the Prime Minister, spent the evening discussing the strategy of the air war, had had a somewhat unnerving experience about getting into the wrong bath in the morning, and, after listening to radio reports of the night's raids, had breakfasted with General Ismay and Admiral Towers. 'After breakfast, Admiral Towers and I both had to go to the *johnny*. The door was one of those cumbersome affairs with locks dating back to Elizabethan times. I had no trouble, but Admiral Towers couldn't get out. He called to me in great consternation to come and help him. Thirty-odd years before, he had contributed to the invention of aviation's first safety belt, but it couldn't aid him now.

'I called the valet. He called the plumbers, the carpenters and the chambermaids. It was Sunday, and they were all down at the pub in the village.

'A bit later, with Mrs. Churchill, I was walking in the garden when to our surprise we saw first the feet, then the blue uniform trousers, and finally the full uniform of an American admiral climbing out of a window on the first floor of Chequers Castle. Mrs. Churchill said, "My, what an extraordinary way to leave the house!" '

According to General Arnold, Prime Minister Churchill was in bed dictating while this was going on. Unlike the smallest rooms of at least one of his predecessors, it may be supposed that those at Chequers at least yielded up no careless secrets, even to an imprisoned admiral. Lord North, British Prime Minister (1770–82), at the time of the War of Independence, when the possibility of American guests in the house was, to say the least of it, unlikely, was singularly careless about his smallest room. Of him, Sir N. William Wraxall, Bart., recorded: 'I have heard a Member of his Cabinet say that it was dangerous to trust him with State papers, which he perpetually mislaid or forgot. A Letter of the first political importance, addressed to him by the King, which he had lost, after a long search was found lying wide open in the water-closet.'

Events under North's administration were recalled by the late Chester Wilmot, quoting the regimental account of the experience of a boatload of the 116th U.S. Infantry when their assault craft was lowered from their 'mother ship' into an unfriendly sea twelve miles off shore during the Normandy landings in 1944: 'Major Dallas's command party made their start under inauspicious circumstances. In lowering the boats from the davits of H.M.S. *Empire Javelin*, the command boat became stuck for 30 minutes directly under the outlet of the ship's "heads" and could go neither up nor down. During this half-hour the ship's company made the most of an opportunity that Englishmen have sought since 1776.'

Thus the catastrophes attending smallest rooms are not by any means confined to being locked in one, or, worse still, locked out. In former times they were sometimes in fact concerned with something more real than mere social discomfort. 'Had a fine accident,' wrote Sylas Neville in his diary in 1771, 'going into the little-house ten guineas which I had put into my watch-pocket on the left side dropped out while I sat. 4 of them fell into the vault. Was obliged to send for a carpenter & have the seat taken up. . . . At last all were found, tho' I had given over 2 of them. More lucky in getting over this accident than I am commonly, God be praised. He knows I could ill afford to lose a guinea.'

It was not, alas, only guineas, but also their owners who suffered. One of the many to endure this fate and be saved was David Hume, the sceptical philosopher, who, according to the diary of Sir Walter Scott's friend, Mrs. Hughes of Uffington: 'built the 2nd house in what is now called St. David's street . . . The North Loch was the receptacle for the drainings and filth of the whole town and though filled with shallow water had at bottom a deep deposit of the blackest and most offensive mud: on his return from inspecting the building of his house, Hume slipt into this dainty slough, and was extricated by three old women, but not till they had exorcised the Atheist as they thought him, by making him say the Lord's Prayer.'

Possibly the greatest number of distinguished people to share this really dreadful kind of catastrophe were those, including eight ruling princes, summoned to a Diet in the Great Hall at Erfurt by the Emperor Frederick I in 1184. The Rev. Nathaniel Wanley, relying on earlier authorities, tells in his *Wonders of the Little World* what befell: 'The emperor . . . had occasion to go to the privy, whither he was followed by some of the nobles, when suddenly the floor that was under them began to sink; the emperor immediately took hold of the iron grates of a window, whereat he hung by the hands till some came and succoured him. Some gentlemen fell to the bottom where they perished. And it is most observable, that amongst those who died was Henry earl of

Schwartzenburg, who carried the presage of his death in a common imprecation of his, which was this, *If I do it not, I wish I may sink in a privy.'*

A presage of death in this sad story persuades me to mention that our smallest rooms have not gone unhaunted. Mr. Anthony Powell, the present literary editor of *Punch,* in his life of John Aubrey, the miscellanist, brought to light this imposing experience (here given in modern English) of Dr. William Twisse of Newbury (1574–1646): 'His son Dr. Twisse, minister of the new church near Tothill Street, Westminster, told me that he had heard his father say that when he was a schoolboy at Winton College that he was a rascal and that one of his schoolfellows and comrades (as wild as himself) died there; and that his father going in the night to the house of office, the phantom or ghost of his dead schoolfellow appeared to him and told him "I am damned"; and that this was the beginning of his conversion.'

Finally, let me select just one of the catastrophes of the Island Race—if that may without offence include the Scots—in distant tropical parts. Charles Waterton in his *Wanderings in South America* (1825) tells of a discomfort far more painful and lasting than that of Mr. Fleet: 'Now in the British plantations of Guiana, as well as in Europe, there is always a little temple dedicated to the goddess Cloacina. Our dinner had chiefly consisted of crabs dressed in rich and different ways. Paumaron is famous for crabs, and strangers who go thither consider them the greatest luxury. The Scottish gentleman made a very capital dinner on crabs; but this change of diet was productive of unpleasant circumstances: he awoke in the night in that state in which Virgil describes Caeleno to have been, viz. "*faedissima ventris proluvies.*" Up he got to verify the remark.' *Serius aut citius, sedem properamus ad unam.*

'Now, unluckily for himself and the nocturnal tranquillity of the planter's house, just at that unfortunate hour the coushie-ants were passing across the seat of Cloacina's temple. He had never dreamed of this; and so, turning his face to the door, he placed himself in the usual situation which the votaries of the goddess generally take. Had a lighted match dropped upon a pound of gunpowder, as he afterwards remarked, it could not have caused a greater recoil. Up he jumped and forced his way out, roaring for help and for a light, for he was worried alive by ten thousand devils. The fact is he had sat down upon an intervening body of coushie-ants. Many of those which escaped being crushed to death turned again, and in revenge stung the unintentional intruder most severely.'

One should not let this subject pass without referring to the jokers whose speciality is contrivance of catastrophe. Some of these stop at musical doors or seats. Others have been more ambitious—such as the wag depicted by Stanley Walker in *Mrs. Astor's Horse.* 'And there is a nameless fellow in Hollywood, an incurable prankster, who has designed an outdoor house to which he likes his guests to retire. As soon as the guest flushes the toilet, an elaborate mechanical device is set in operation, causing the walls of the house to open and fall to the ground, much like the opening of the petals of a beautiful flower, leaving the victim of the jest exposed to the howls of the host and the other guests.'

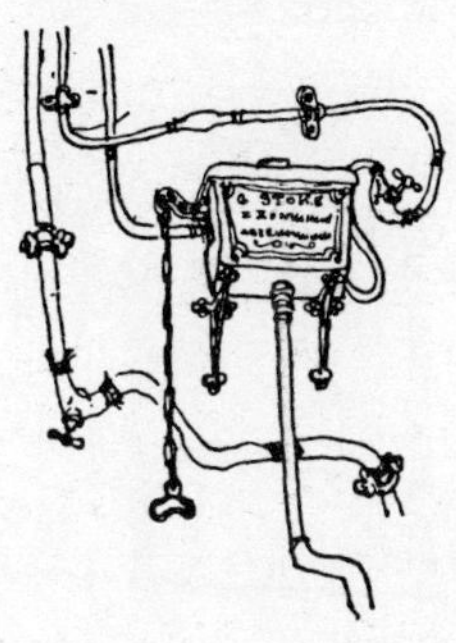

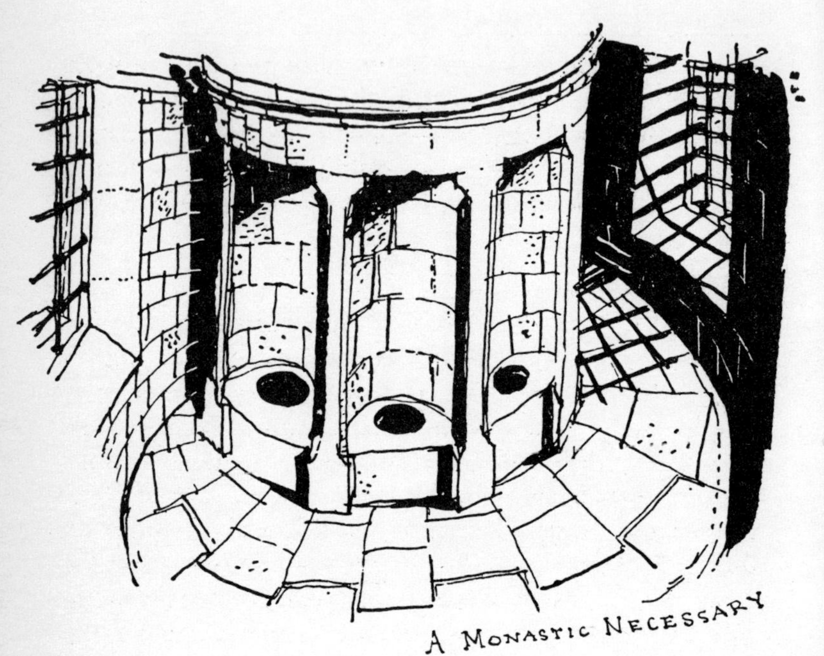

A Monastic Necessary

Royal Flush

ROYAL EUPHEMISMS—DEATH IN THE CLOSET—ROMAN EMPERORS AND THE SEA-KINGS OF KNOSSOS—MR. FLEET IN THE GREEK ISLANDS—A ROYAL TYPHOID CASE—MEDIEVAL ARRANGEMENTS—QUEEN ANNE—THE HANOVERIANS — EUROPEAN ROYALTY — THE WHERRY-GO-NIMBLES OF GEORGE IV—AN EMINENT VICTORIAN

THIS delicate subject of royalty and the smallest room is not without social significance; for quite diverse, and sometimes even republican, peoples specifically refer to royalty when they use polite phrases for their smallest rooms. The French speak of *aller ou le roi va à pied.* The Bulgarians, long Tzar-less, still speak regally of *kadeto i Tzara hodi pesha*—going where even the Tzar goes on foot. The royalist Danes excuse themselves with *At gå hvor selv Kongen gar alene*, referring to the place where the king goes alone.

This implication of regal solitariness must be relatively modern, for Madame de Maintenon, we are told on the authority of the Duke de St. Simon, frequently accompanied Louis Quatorze to his garde-robe. At least one sovereign, the Emperor Charles V of Spain, was born, and not a few have come to their ends, in a smallest room. There was our own George II, for instance, the last British monarch to lead his soldiers in battle, whose demise was described by Horace Walpole in a letter to George Montagu in 1760: 'He went to bed well last night, rose at six this morning as usual, looked, I suppose, if all his money was in his purse, and called for his chocolate. A little after seven, he went into the water-closet; the German *valet de chambre* heard a noise, listened, heard something like a groan, ran in, and found the hero of Oudenarde and Dettingen on the floor, with a gash on his right temple, by falling against the corner of a bureau. He tried to speak, could not, and expired.'

We must concede, in spite of a morbid note of wonder that sometimes creeps in, that monarchs are human, and have much in common with the rest of mankind. This was expressed bluntly enough by the Scots poet Alexander Barclay in 1515 when he was a monk at Ely, before he became rector of All Hallows, in Lombard Street in the City of London, in the somewhat trite lines:

> The lordes siege and rurall mens ordure
> Be like of savour.

Scriptural anecdotes of early royalty's somewhat melancholy experiences of jakes are noticed by Sir John Harington in his light display of grave learning that we shall examine in another chapter. The first occurs in the third chapter of Judges where it is told how the left-handed Ehud rose up to deliver the children of Israel out of their eighteen years' bondage to that 'very fat man,' Eglon, king of Moab. Ehud came upon Eglon when the latter, according to our Authorized Version, was in 'a summer parlour' where he 'covered his feet' and Ehud thereupon thrust his dagger into the Moabite's quilted belly. In the second instance, recorded in I Samuel 24, David 'cut off the skirt of Saul's robe privily' in a cave where he, too, had gone 'to cover his feet.' The euphemism is obvious. The Latin of the Vulgate is more explicit and may be plainly Englished 'to void his belly.'

As Richard Codrington in *The Mirror of History*[1] in 1653 somewhat sententiously observes: 'Strange kinds of deaths happen upon Princes more than on any other men. . . . Divers have been slain in the draught.'[2] He then instances 'that beast Heliogabalus, whom Rome so hated,' as being 'killed upon his stool at easement, and thrown into Tyber,' and adds 'Gneius Garbo, a man of great dignity and power in Rome, was commanded that he should be slain, as he was sitting on his stool of ease, by Pompey, in the third time of his Consulship in Rome.'

The same Nathaniel Wanley who recorded the catastrophe of the Emperor Frederick I also cites as an example of the prodigious luxury of the profligate Heliogabalus that 'his excrements he discharged into gold vessels, and urined into vessels of onyx, or myrrhine pots . . . and even these, and the most part of his other vessels had lascivious engravings represented on the sides of them.'

The policy of some other Roman emperors in matters of sanitation was somewhat less self-indulgent. Titus Tacius, who reigned with Romulus,

[1] I was pleased to notice, irrelevantly, that the book was printed 'near the Upper Pump.'

[2] One of Shakespeare's words for privy—used in *Timon* and in *Troilus*.

erected a statue of the drain-goddess Cloacina in what has been described as 'a goodly large house of office, a fit shrine for such a saint.'

The Emperor Vespasian built sumptuous smallest rooms for his subjects and, moreover, insisted upon their being used. 'Of his princely bounty and magnificence,' the record tells us, he 'erected diverse places of fair polished marble, for this special purpose, requiring and no less straightly charging all persons, as well citizens as strangers, to refrain from all other places, saving these specially appointed.'

But a flushing closet was a perquisite of royalty long before the Imperial plumbers of Rome. Perhaps the oldest water-closet to survive the ravages of the barbarians who from time to time sweep aside what is wholesome and civilized in human achievement, is that discovered by the late Sir Arthur Evans in the Palace of the Sea-Kings at Knossos. In the private apartments of this great Minoan Palace in Crete was discovered a little bathroom and, beside it, a smallest room which Evans described thus: 'On the face of a gypsum slab . . . is a groove for a seat about 57 cm. from the floor. Outside the doorway of the latrine is a flag (stone) sloped towards a semicircular hole, forming a sink, and from this opens a small duct leading to the main drain. The aperture leading to the main drain, partly masked by a curious projection, deviates from the centre of the seat, thus leaving room . . . for some vessel used for flushing the basin.'

Leonard Cottrell, describing in *The Bull of Minos* his own exploration of this ancient place, notes a characteristic twentieth-century reverence for this oldest smallest room: 'It is typical of our technological age that, for most lay visitors to the Knossian Palace, none of its aesthetic treasures make such a profound appeal as this 3,600-year-old latrine. Indeed, for anyone to whom sanitation and civilization are synonymous, Knossos is irresistible. It is a Plumber's Paradise.'

A sad thought I must mention in passing is that in the course of his many years at sea, Mr. Fleet actually paid a visit to the shores of Crete without being aware of the existence of this unique shrine. He recalls a local wine attacking his faculties, leaving the memory of a sunny blur tinged with a sense of indignation and nausea at a little stinking iron erection on the quayside 'which ought to have been condemned and would have been done away with in any self-respecting country.' Mr. Fleet sighed over this lost opportunity. 'Nobody told me about no kings, living or dead, and if anybody had spoken of there being drains in this here place you mention, I wouldn't have believed them, and that's straight.'

It was many a long dark century before British monarchy could aspire to anything like the comforts enjoyed by the sea-kings of Knossos, three thousand years before Christ. It was indeed only a few generations ago that the heir to the British throne came near to losing his life through bad sanitation of the kind Mr. Fleet so greatly deplored in the Greek islands. In October, 1871, the Prince of Wales, afterwards King Edward VII, stayed with his friends, the Earl and Countess of Londesborough, at Londesborough Lodge, near Scarborough. Soon after this visit, on his return to Sandringham, he went down with typhoid, obviously contracted at Londesborough, for both the Earl of Chesterfield, who had also been of the party, and the Prince's groom, who had been with his master, sickened and died. The Prince lay for a month weakening under the strain of the fever, and for a while his life was despaired of. Then he rallied and, at length in the following February, though 'pale as yet and feverworn,' he drove with the Queen to a thanksgiving service at St. Paul's amid such an uprush of public emotion as placed the monarchy on a firmer basis than it had been for at least a decade.

Clearly the Prince's illness was due to bad drainage. Since the latter end of the eighteenth century, it had become usual to fit water-closets inside houses with no ventilation and with unventilated pipes taken into a cesspool. Mephitic gases invaded these houses, with obvious consequences. Improved methods of drainage and better types of fittings were demanded. The national feeling aroused by the Prince's danger at least speeded up the movement for reform. The Prince himself was interested. According to an American writer on sanitary matters, he once declared that were he not a prince he would wish to be a plumber.

In more turbulent times, infection was not by any means the only risk to royal persons visiting their smallest rooms. King Edmund Ironside, only six months after his division of the realm with King Canute in 1016, came to an untimely end in such a place. According to one chronicler, Guydo, treacherous son of Edricus, 'awaytynge his time, espyed when the kynge was at the withdraught to purge nature, and with a spere strake hym into the foundement, and so into the body; wherof kyng Edmunde dyed shortly after . . .'

It is not perhaps surprising that monarchs did not choose to go unattended on their private affairs. It may indeed have been a prudent desire for self-preservation that initiated the cherished and, to a modern mind, somewhat doubtful privilege of accompanying the sovereign to the privy. From this practice, no doubt, arose the custom of granting formal audiences in a smallest room, an example, as we shall see later, sometimes followed by eminent persons not of royal blood.

In the English royal household, the fortunate holder of this privilege was described as the Groom or Yeoman of the stole chamber, or wardrobe, which was originally no more than the room containing the king's close-stool. Latterly, the office was confined to the care of the sovereign's ceremonial robes, but there is no doubt that in an earlier period it included more intimate service. The style of the office, having undergone several changes, still survives. Under Charles II, the bearer became Master of the Great Wardrobe, then housed in Wardrobe Place in the City; under Edward VII, Gentleman Usher of the Robes; under Edward VIII, Master of the Robes, and under George VI, Groom of the Robes.

Our third Henry, whose long reign began in 1216, was a great patron of the arts and delighted to oversee the details of the building carried out for him. We find him in 1238 ordering the Constable of the Tower to 'cause the drain of our privy chamber to be made in the fashion of a hollow column' and, thirty years later, dictating that the privy chamber of the queen's room in Winchester Castle should be made 'in the fashion of a turret with double vaulting.' His concern for the seemliness of his smallest rooms is perhaps best shown in a letter which he wrote to Edward FitzOtho, his Master of the Works, in 1245: 'Since the privy chamber of our wardrobe at London is situated in an unsuitable place, wherefore it smells badly, we command you, on the faith and love by which you are bound to us, that you in no wise omit to cause another privy chamber to be made in the same wardrobe in such more fitting and proper place as you may select there, even though it should cost a hundred pounds.'

It must have been in an evil-smelling place that Richard III dwelt upon his stratagems. When Brackenbury, Constable of the Tower, refused to carry out the crooked-back usurper's designs against his nephews, a royal page put forward the name of Tyrell. Then, says Holinshed, 'vpon this pages words king Richard arose, for this communication had he sitting at the draught, a convenient carpet for such a councell,' and briefed the odious Tyrell for his horrid business.

Scottish thrones were not without their moments of insecurity. The first James of Scotland came to an untimely end in a monastic privy at Perth in 1437. The sixteenth-century accounts of the Lord High

Treasurer of Scotland include a number of payments made for close-stools for his more fortunate successors. In 1501, eightpence was given for a stool of ease for King James IV, and nearly five times that canny sum for two-and-three-quarter ells of white cloth with which to cover it. In 1505, John Forman was reimbursed for the nineteen shillings and tenpence he had paid for 'a great stool of ease' at Dumbarton and, some time afterwards, five shillings for another 'in the Kingis schip.'

But these would seem to have been austere contraptions compared with those affected by the young James V, who came to the throne a year-old infant in 1513 and died in 1542. In 1538, the year of his second marriage, to Mary of Lorraine, fifteen-and-a-half ells of green damask were used in making a pavilion for the king's stool of ease, and since this supposedly splendid fabric was three pounds fifteen shillings the ell (of a given forty-five inches) the total cost was £58 2s. 6d. Only a little less expensive were the two-and-a-half ells of 'tanny velvet' at fifty-five shillings the ell which were delivered in 1540 'to cover ane stule of eis of the King's gracis for the schip.'

The Tudors seem to have sat no less softly than the Stuarts. That great authority on furniture, Mr. R. W. Symonds, has drawn attention[1] to the hitherto-unremarked family of Grene or Greene, coffer-makers, who, on the evidence of the royal household accounts, made a variety of things, including many close-stools, for the royal palaces throughout the

[1] 'The Craft of the Coffer Maker' in *The Connoisseur*, March 1941.

sixteenth century. One example of these stools, made in 1547, was for 'the vse of the kynges mageste;' it was, says Mr. Symonds, 'covered with black velvet and garnished with ribbon and nails and fringes. The seat and elbows were covered with white "fuschan" filled with down; 2,000 gilt nails for garnishing were used and the stool was supplied with two leather cases lined with black cotton and fitted with girdles—one for the stool and the other for the bowl and the "sesstornes." The leather case would signify that this luxurious stool accompanied Henry VIII on his travels.' The close-stool was clearly a movable article of furniture and not a fitting.

Formerly supported on legs, it was more often made in Tudor times like a trunk with a lid. One such, belonging to about 1600, on which either Elizabeth or James I or both in succession may have sat, is still preserved at Hampton Court. This is covered in crimson velvet, bound and panelled with lace secured by gilt-headed nails. There is a handle, for lifting and carrying, at either side. The locked curved lid opens to display a pierced and velvet-padded seat, under which a basin, of china, pewter, or even silver, was set.

But an end of such contrivances in general was foreshadowed by Sir John Harington, godson of Queen Elizabeth I, to whom we still have to pay tribute in another chapter. Harington built what was probably the first water-closet in England, and in 1596 published his merry *Metamorphosis of Ajax* describing and illustrating the device. Perhaps the queen was amused. She was at least impressed sufficiently to have one of the new contrivances installed at Richmond Palace, with a copy of Harington's book chained to the wall therein; and she sent him her 'thankes for the inuention.'

But, alas, the queen's example was little followed either by her subjects or her Stuart successors. Anthony à Wood, the Oxford antiquary, records in his diary, after Charles II and his court had spent most of the summer of 1665 in Oxford to avoid the plague in London: 'though they were neat and gay in their apparell, yet they were very nasty and beastly, leaving at their departure their excrements in every corner, in chimneys, studies, colehouses, cellers. Rude, rough, whoremongers; vaine, empty, careless.'

The chill arrangements made at Windsor for Charles's niece Anne were inspected with interest by the intrepid Celin Fiennes who journeyed through England on a side-saddle at the turn of the seventeenth century. In notes written between 1708 and 1713, she describes the dressing-room of the consort, Prince George of Denmark: 'Within the dressing room is a Closet on one hand, the other side is a Closet that leads to a little place with a seat of Easement of Marble with sluices of water to wash all down.'

The Hanoverians prompt one more irresistible piece of tattle from Horace Walpole, reporting on the coronation of George III. 'The Coronation is over. 'tis even a more gorgeous sight than I imagined. . . . Of all the incidents of the day, the most diverting was what happened to the Queen. She had a retiring-chamber, with *all* conveniences, prepared behind the altar. She went thither—in the *most convenient* what found she but—the Duke of Newcastle!'

Walpole's arch enjoyment of the royal contretemps derives from the fact that certain things were then done secretly in England and seldom mentioned in polite society except euphemistically, a contrast to Continental habits which his younger contemporary, Sir N. William Wraxall, was quick to point out. Wraxall, touring Europe as a young man, formed a friendship with Sir William and the first, and more respectable, Lady Hamilton at Naples in 1779. He was thus enabled to collect information about the observances of the court of Ferdinand IV of Naples. 'Those acts and functions which are never mentioned in England,' he wrote, 'and which are there studiously concealed, even by the vulgar, here are openly performed. When the King has made a hearty meal, and feels an inclination to retire, he commonly communicates that intention to the Noblemen around him in waiting, and selects the favoured individuals, whom, as a mark of predilection, he chooses shall attend him. "*Sono ben pransato,*" says he, laying his hand on his belly, "*Adesso bisogna un buona panchiata.*" The persons thus preferred, then accompany his Majesty, stand respectfully round him, and amuse him by their conversation, during the performance.'

To this information derived from the Hamiltons, Sir Nathaniel adds a learned gloss of his own which no student of that which pertains to the smallest room can afford to ignore. 'However strong this fact may appear, and however repugnant to our ideas of decency; it has been for successive centuries, perfectly consonant to the manners of the Italians in general, and scarcely less so to those of the French. D'Aubigné, a grave writer, in the "*Memoirs of His Own Life,*" does not hesitate to relate in the most circumstantial manner, the narrow escape which Henry the Fourth, his master, had of being knocked on the head, while engaged in this necessary function. Nay, D'Aubigné composed a "*Quatrain*" on the adventure, which he has transmitted to posterity. The story is so naturally related, and is so characteristic of the nation, that I can't resist giving it in the words of the author, which I shall not however venture to translate. Henry, who was then only King of Navarre, having effected his escape from Paris, in 1575, on which occasion D'Aubigné accompanied him; they passed the River Seine at Poissy, and soon afterwards stopped to refresh themselves in a village. Here, says D'Aubigné, the king "*etant allé faire ses affaires dans un tet à cochons, une vielle qui le surprit en cet état, lui auroit fendue la tête par derrière, d'un coup de Serpe, sans moi qui parai le coup.*" It is clear from this circumstance that D'Aubigné must have been close to his royal master at the time. Then follows the ludicrous Epitaph which he made for the occasion, on a supposition that the old woman had killed the king.

"Cy git un Roi, grand par merveille,
Qui mourut comme Dieu permet,
D'un coup de serpe d'un vielle,
Ainsi qui'l chioit dans un tet."

'His predecessor, Henry the Third, it is well known, was stabbed in the belly, of which wound he died, in 1589, while sitting on the *Chaise percée*;

in which indecorous situation he did not scruple to give audience to Clement, the regicide Monk, who assassinated him. Marshal Suarrow, in our own time, received his Aids du Camp and his General Officers, precisely in a similar manner. Madame de Maintenon, as the Duke de St. Simon informs us, thought those moments so precious, that she commonly accompanied Louis the Fourteenth to the "Garderobe." So did Louvois, when Minister of State. The Duke de Vendôme, while commanding the Armies of France in Spain and Italy, at the commencement of the last Century, was accustomed to receive the greatest personages, on public business, in the same situation. We have Cardinal Alberoni's authority for this fact. If we read the account written by Du Bois, of the last illness of Louis the Thirteenth, we may there see what humiliating functions Anne of Austria performed for that Prince in the course of his malady; over which, an English writer, more fastidious, would have drawn a veil. Mademoiselle de Montpensier, and the Palatine Duchess of Orléans, though women of the highest birth and rank, as well as of unimpeached conduct, conceal nothing on these points, in their writings. The former, speaking of the Duchess of Orléans, her step-mother, second wife of Gaston, brother of Louis the Thirteenth, says, "She had contracted a singular habit of always running into another room, *pour se placer sur la Chaise percée*, when dinner was announced. As she never failed in this particular, the Grand Maître, or Lord Steward of Gaston's Household, who performed the ceremony of summoning their Royal Highnesses to table; observed, smelling to his Baton of office, that there must certainly be either Senna or Rhubarb in its composition, as it invariably produced the effect of sending the Duchess to the Garderobe." I have, myself, seen the late Electress Dowager of Saxony, daughter of the Emperor Charles the Seventh, at her own palace, in the suburbs of Dresden, rise from the table where she was playing, when the room has been full of company of both sexes; lay down her cards, retire for a few minutes, during which time the game was suspended, and then return, observing to those near her, "*J'ai pris Médécine aujourd'huy.*" These circumstances sufficiently prove that Ferdinand, however gross his manners or language seem to us, by no means shocked the feelings, or excited the disgust of his own courtiers.'

Medicine was an embarrassment to our own George IV, or, more characteristically, to others on his behalf, when he visited Ireland in 1821. Creevey rattles off the story: 'But lo! the wherry-go-nimbles, which had so unreasonably attacked the Royal stomach (for even Kings are subject to these unkingly complaints) gave His Majesty full employment at the Phoenix Park, and the Duke of Leinster arrived at the Curragh with this direful intelligence.

'Lord Portarlington and the other Stewards, 12 in number, were assembled to receive this 2nd. St. Patrick. They had spent nearly £5,000 in erecting a glass house and providing a suitable banquet for the Royal party. When, therefore, they were informed of the complaint which detained their promised guest, their grief was audible, but they were in some measure comforted by the assurance, that if the

Castor Oil (so liberally administered) was true to its office, he would come on Friday, the day but one after.

'One of the Stewards stood forth with great solemnity in the august assembly of Managers and said, "Gentlemen, I fear one thing has been omitted, which it appears may be an essential *necessary*, I mean a watercloset, and I humbly propose that Artists may be forthwith summoned from Dublin to erect one before his arrival." '

Nevertheless, it took more than royal attacks of wherry-go-nimbles and the employment of 'Artists' —which seems to have been a euphemism for the Mr. Fleets of the period—to improve conditions in Britain's royal palaces. It took that enlightened and persistent reformer, Albert, Prince Consort. There was room for improvement. In 1844, no less than fifty-three overflowing cesspools were discovered under Windsor Castle. The Prince Consort with characteristic energy attacked the sorry state of affairs, replacing Hanoverian commodes with up-to-date water-closets. But, alas, with his death there was a tendency to accept the *status quo* in sanitation as in everything else, so that all might remain as it had been in his lifetime, all in some degree part of one great Albert memorial.

It was not until ten years after his death that the typhoid of the heir to the throne awakened the national conscience to the perils of its smallest rooms and its noisome drains, the reform of which had for years been strenuously urged by such sanitary pioneers as Edwin Chadwick, whose good works were somewhat belatedly acknowledged with a knighthood in the eighteen-eighties.

That an era of serious plumbing had been established at last is indicated in an absorbing account of the eminent firm of Dent and Hellyer, whose fortunes were greatly supplemented by the new Victorian outlook toward plumbing. The story, written by Mr. Bertram Hellyer in 1930 on the occasion of the firm's bi-centenary, is called *Under Eight Reigns*, and records the activities of his firm from George I to George V. His Victorian forebear, S. S. Hellyer, came near to being honoured by the great Queen herself, thus demonstrating the new esteem in which his craft was held. 'We have it on good authority that he was recommended for a knighthood, but it was only in keeping with his general modesty that he should have declined this honour.'

Hellyer's modesty did not cramp his style when he lectured in London in the eighteen-eighties. It may indeed be fitting to round off our survey of royalty in the smallest room with a visionary and resounding peroration spoken by this worthy Holder of Royal Warrants. 'Lying there in those strong arms of yours, slumbering in the hardened muscles, resting in the well-trained fingers and educated hands, lies the health of this leviathan city. The plumber's part in making a house, a town, a city healthy is enormous. Let the plumbing be done on the principles laid down in these lectures, and this huge city, teeming though it be with human beings, will become the healthiest, as it is now the greatest, city in the world.' Not even Mr. Fleet at his most eloquent, fortified by a respectful audience and by a decent libation of old ale, could wind up to greater effect.

Accessories and Fancies

THE PRINCE CONSORT'S ECONOMIES AT WINDSOR CASTLE —QUEEN VICTORIA HOODWINKED AT CAMBRIDGE— DYLAN THOMAS ON TOILET PAPER—SQUARES OR ROLLS? —THE NERVOUS AIR PASSENGER—TOILET PAPER AND THE YOUNG—ITS INVENTION AND PROMOTION—ITS PREDECESSORS—FANCIFUL SMALLEST ROOMS—THEIR DECORATION AND OUTLOOK

THE double use of reading matter taken into a smallest room, first as food for the mind and then for what Lord Chesterfield termed 'a sacrifice to Cloacina' has already been commended. Now, before we dismiss princes and palaces from these pages, it might be mentioned that the Prince Consort's arrangements—and economies—at Windsor Castle persisted long after he was gone, in affording this dual satisfaction. When the Prince of Wales, afterwards Edward VII, occupied the Castle for a while in 1892, one of his equerries wrote with nice facetiousness to the Queen's private secretary: 'We are fairly comfortable in this most conveniently built house. . . . We all admire various little economical thrifty dodges here. In the W.C.s—NEWSPAPER squares—there was one idea of sending them to Cowell in an unpaid envelope . . .'

The official threatened with postage due was Sir John Cowell, Master of the Household, and as such charged with maintaining the *status quo* in all things, and one unlikely to yield to protest over the thrifty dodges of the long-lamented Albert. It may be assumed therefore that guests in the smallest rooms at Royal Windsor continued to enjoy the common luxury of reading newsprint well into the present century.

On one occasion at least, Queen Victoria herself was actually confronted with the evidence of such sacrifices of her subjects to Cloacina. In *Period Piece*, that dulcet, atmospheric account of her Cambridge childhood, Gwen Raverat recalls a foul Cam and a shrewd Queen who for once was hoodwinked: 'I can remember the smell very well, for all the sewage went into the river, till the town was at last properly drained, when I was about ten years old. There is a tale of Queen Victoria being shown over Trinity by the Master, Dr. Whewell, and saying, as she looked down over the bridge: "What are all those pieces of paper floating down the river?" To which, with great presence of mind, he replied: "Those, ma'am, are notices that bathing is forbidden." '

The very usage of the impolite euphemism *bumf* suggests not only something that should be read and discarded (the popular view in the armed forces), but also something upon which to write: and it must be admitted that toilet paper has served many useful purposes in the opposite sense to that intended, namely, as a vehicle of self-expression.

Fertile imagination or graphic memory—none of us, alas, will ever know now—prompted Dylan Thomas in his *Portrait of the Artist as a Young Dog* to make a suggestion that might perhaps have delighted, or perhaps outraged, Lord Chesterfield.

Mr. Humphries, the school teacher, writer of an unsuccessful novel, wanted to know 'Why don't they have serials on matchboxes?' Mr. Roberts, a disreputable man of middle age, said: 'No, Mr. Humphries, on toilet rolls would be best.' Mr. Roberts then went on to recollect staying in a London surburb with a couple called Armitage: 'He made curtains and blinds. They used to leave each other messages on the toilet paper every single day.'

Books, poems, love letters, vital messages of all kinds, as well as ribaldries have been written on the stuff by prisoners, captives, and all manner of men taken short by circumstances and by those emotionally constrained. A world-renowned composer, who will, I think, prefer to remain anonymous in this context, told me that he made lavish use of the ship's issue of the stuff for his creative jottings while crossing the Atlantic in the grim conditions of a wartime transport vessel—and what a proud collector's piece these humble sheets will make!

Officialdom, with which somehow the article is hopelessly entangled, had its own special fling when at Croydon Airport it produced toilet paper stamped with the legend AIR MINISTRY PROPERTY—NOT TO BE TAKEN AWAY. Private individuals and commercial enterprises have equally left their mark. The loyal ardour of a well-meaning manufacturer had to be restrained when he sought to issue toilet paper bearing the portraits of their late Majesties King George V and Queen Mary to celebrate their Jubilee.

From Hollywood I hear that that almost regal old-timer Tom Mix had everything monogrammed including toilet paper, and I am sure there are many noble and even royal families who have followed his example.

'I take it you're going to have squares, not rolls?' said Mr. Fleet in one of those critical moments when our smallest room seemed on the point of completion and when he himself had nothing further to offer than advice of a somewhat compelling kind.

The average citizen, faced with a quandary like this, might well make a snap decision as I was forced to do, abandoning a childish predilection for all the funny things that happen with rolls, to acknowledge without conviction the sternly progressive views of Mr. Fleet that 'for such as goes in for that sort of thing' interleaved packs are the thing.

A simple enough decision, this, for an individual, commanding all the wonders of the age short of extravagant caprice, in establishing a smallest room like ours on terra firma. How different for those who have to provide airborne comforts and to learn their lessons from such incidents as this, passed on to me by an airline operator: 'A nervous passenger was occupying the small room of a DC-3 (and it was small indeed on these aircraft), when rough weather was encountered. In accordance with regulations the "Return to Seat" sign was switched on, and our passenger, fearing something untoward was afoot, acted with more haste than discretion, with the result that the end of the roll got tucked in the top of his trousers. As he fled down the gangway to his seat,

the train of paper was greeted with roars of laughter from the other passengers and our friend was embarrassed and annoyed. As a result of a complaint he made, rolls were abandoned by the airline and interleaved sheets substituted.'

The main distinction, perhaps, between what Mr. Fleet contrasts as squares and rolls is not a matter of social snobbery, as he would have us believe, but rather one of humour. Whereas there is nothing funny about squares, there is everything in rolls that appeals to an irresponsible sense of humour (probably clever men would call it a *release of taboo*) lurking in people of all ages. It is most marked in schoolboys and undergraduates. Soon after the British schoolboy settles down to his years of exile at expensive boarding schools, he encounters the wag who releases a streamer of toilet paper from the train bearing the expensively educated little scholars away from school. I say *away* from school because the gesture is one of emotional release. It never happens on the journey toward school when our young learn to wear a stiff upper lip and when the mood is emotionally tense, even apprehensive.

Fred Bickerton, who as a college porter had ample opportunities to reflect upon gilded youth at Oxford, wrote, after his retirement: 'Toilet paper . . . has a magic power over undergraduates. On festive occasions in one college, the place used to be festooned from tower to tower with it. I have seen decorations made of it hung from beam to beam in our Dining Hall at University College, and also "nudes" after Bump Suppers dancing round bonfires in the quad, tastefully draped in this material.'

Who invented the stuff? There is some confusion about the only begetter of toilet paper as such, but there seems little doubt that the perforated roll was a child of the inventive flair of Walter James Alcock, the Victorian pioneer, who in the eighteen-eighties took over a bankrupt concern when the demand for toilet paper was limited by what his descendants have called the 'prudish attitude' of the public. Alcock at first found it an uphill task of promotion. Chemists could be persuaded to stock the unmentionable article but only under the counter. To display it was considered 'daring.' Nor would customers in those days actually ask for it, preferring to shelter behind the euphemism *curl papers*. It is possible, indeed, that the stuff originated from those essential nineteenth-century aids to adornment in the same way that cleaning tissues and paper handkerchiefs in the twentieth century have given rise, so they tell me in the trade, to *de luxe* two-ply rolls much favoured by the very rich, by hygiene-obsessed Americans, and by babies—who, it must be granted, have little choice in the matter.

Walter James Alcock's pioneering efforts to overcome prudery in his customers and to extend the use of his products were, of course, rewarded, and the London works he founded now export their comforts to forty-two countries.

Not that British demand in these days is unforthcoming. One prominent manufacturer alone, so the statisticians inform me, disposes of twenty thousand tons in Britain every year, this notwithstanding the fact that a modest roll in happier days costing sixpence, now, at the time of writing, costs 1s. 3d.

The kind of social distinctions which appeal to such politically awakened minds as that of Mr. Fleet, still linger in the trade. Superior brands called 'sulphite' are generally marketed by chemists. The less refined and cheaper lines of 'crepe' paper go over the counters of grocery and hardware stores. In canny Scotland, there are sometimes minor controversies about the number of sheets in a roll or a pack. Protesting customers, perhaps to while away their moments of ease in their smallest rooms, or perhaps to feel that they are putting their time to useful purpose, actually carry out counts. It is, I fear, one more case of the rich getting the pleasure. Only the highest quality and most expensive outfits now offer a thousand sheets. The poorer customers must be content with anything from two to seven hundred.

What preceded the douce benison of the paper that to-day so many of us take for granted? It is a subject I prefer not to explore in detail, except to recall that civilized Romans used perfumed wool and sometimes sponges, that medieval laity were known to use curved sticks and bunches of hay, that ecclesiastics, whose smallest rooms were often well found and often communal, seemed to have favoured the shreds and tatters of their own discarded habits. It must be admitted that many Eastern peoples with their sometimes elaborate ablutions have often been found to be more wholesome and cleanly than the peoples of so-called Western civilization. Nor was the almost intolerably uncomfortable (so one would have thought) habit of savage and primitive peoples of using stones unknown to the English-speaking world. An old English quatrain, too lewd for these pages, but authentic enough, shows that the use of stones was not uncommon among the shepherds of the Sussex Downs long after, it is hoped, city folk were learning better.

Apart from the indispensable accessory we have been discussing, there is much thought, folly, human ingenuity and indeed vanity, devoted to the furnishing

of our smallest rooms. Mr. Fleet, won over like many an eminent architect such as the late Sir Edwin Lutyens, to the idea of a bookshelf in such places, objected strenuously to any form of decoration that might distract the user, and, of course, to pictures, which he said 'only serve to take your mind off the proper business of the place.' He seemed to regard our modest scheme of things as an outrageous innovation, an affront to his progressive and puritanical approach to the smallest room.

Yet frivolity, or decorative fancy, in such places, as we pointed out to him, knows not the frontiers of time or place. The marble latrines in the harem of Shah Jahan in Agra built in the seventeenth century ran with water perfumed with otto of roses and were fitted with vases of the perfumed water, which was an early Indian substitute for toilet paper. Both the twentieth-century Hollywood and medieval Europe have expressed some gay foibles in the arrangement of their smallest rooms.

Let me invoke once more the immortal spirit of Dylan Thomas, and that schoolroom conversation of his during the drawing class when inaccurate drawings of naked girls were surreptitiously passed round: 'What would you do if you had a million pounds?' Some would buy a Bugatti, a Rolls-Royce, or a harem; some would buy a cricket or a football field, a garage complete with mechanics and lift, or all the railway trains, or cigarettes with real gold tips. . . . But there was one who plumped for 'A lavatory as big as, as big as the Melba Pavilion, with plush seats and golden chains and . . .'

What a wealth of human invention has gone into the furnishing of privies. A mile or so away from me as I write, is the fanciful place at Knole, the walls of which one or other of the Sackvilles caused to be entirely papered with postage stamps bearing the image of Queen Victoria and varnished over all, this fancy it is said was for the delectation of Edward VII when he was the guest beneath that hospitable roof. Though the commode used by King James I, and richly enchased silver toilet utensils prepared for his visit are on view to the public, this charming postage-stamp fancy remains hidden from sightseeing in a private part of the great house.

From Hollywood come many vivid accounts of twentieth-century splendour. 'I have visions,' writes my correspondent, somewhat breathlessly, of a reigning film actress's smallest room 'having a soft luxurious carpet from wall to wall and her downstairs powder room for a long while had a gay circus motif, but she changed it recently. Some stars go in for sunken bathtubs—and tropical plants—the latest craze is the poodle motif—the toilet seats are gay with prancing poodles. The painted seat craze is rampant—some have them monogrammed, others have flower motifs—some go in for galloping horses.'

This correspondent rattles on about ermine mats and mink-covered seats, fancies which might be taken with a pinch of salt were it not for the touch of authenticity clipped from the distinguished columnist Kendis Rochlen, billed by her newspaper as 'Candid Kendis,' offering her readers a few Yuletide hints: 'Hand-painted toilet seats are replacing the Marilyn Monroe calendar trays and glasses as the hottest gag gift item in Hollywood this Christmas. But they're an expensive chuckle—they cost $35 per seat.

'I discovered them out in Beverly Hills where they're selling so fast that one exclusive store has had trouble keeping them in stock. And it's not just the Hollywood gang that's tittering over the French phrases and designs that embellish this once-dull accessory of the *chambre de toilette*.

'The sales staff tells me the tricky little lids are going great guns with the society folk, too.

'There's one design that features French poodles prancing around the old rim.

' "This is really for Milady," the saleslady smiled. The lid is lettered "Oui Oui, Madame." There's more art on the bottom of the seat.

'When you lift it up you're greeted with the phrase, "Hello, Bebe!"

'For the gentlemen, there's another version. It features excellent oil paintings of can-can dancers—à la Toulouse Lautrec. "Oo, la la le cabinat," reads the lid. There are more girls and high kicks decorating the rim. Then comes the final gag when you lift the seat.

' "Oo la la, papa—for men only!" says the fancy lettering.

'Oh yes, the painting is guaranteed not to rub off.'

A Sunday issue of the *Los Angeles Times* carried in its Shoppers' Mart column this winsome advertisement, attractively illustrated, for 'Dear John' decorated seats: '12 Colorful Designs. Brighten up your bathroom. Designs for any home. Modern, Circus, Farm House, His and Hers, and many others. Apply these designs yourself—easy as decals —on all 4 sides of your toilet seat. Water and acid proof. Won't rub off. Handy "Dear John" DO-IT-YOURSELF kit only $4.95 with simple instructions to fit all toilet seats. Or send for complete hand decorated seat $19.95. Guaranteed satisfaction. Order from "Dear John," Dept., etc. . . .'

An equally wholesome predilection for décor, untrammelled by theories of hygiene, is reflected in an account written in 1662, describing privies built much earlier in a Nottinghamshire monastery: 'Every Seat, and Partition was of Wainscott, close on either side, so that they could not see one another when they were in that place. There were as many Seats on either side as there were little Windows in the Wall to give light to the said Seats which afterwards were walled up to make the House more close. At the West-end of it there were three fair glass Windows;

which great Windows gave light to the whole House.'

Lest it be supposed that pictures are a contemporary innovation in a smallest room, let me recall *The First and Best Part of Scogins Jests*, gathered by Andrew Boord, Doctor of Physicke . . . 1656. Scogin, they say, was a skilled philosopher, though 'bent to merry devices,' and here is the story of how the French king had Scogin into his house of office and showed him the king of England's picture: 'On a time, when the French King went to his stoole, he did take Scogin with him. Then said the French King to Scogin, "looke behind thee, who is pictured on the wall," Scogin looked, said "it is a faire picture." The King said: "thou maist see what I doe make of a picture of thy king." Scogin beheld the picture of the King of England and said to the French king: "Iesu Christ! Here is a wonderfull thing! What would you doe, if you did see the King of England in the face as he is, when that for feare you do beshit yourselfe, when that you looke but upon a picture of him?" Then the French king banished Scogin out of France, and he came into England againe.'

As the final touches are made to any smallest room, it becomes clear that the ultimate consideration is an aesthetic one. The window is not only a matter of ventilation or even escape. There is the desirability of a view to be reckoned with. This we found locally was a matter of heresy. Mr. Fleet the plumber, Fred the stonemason, George the carpenter, and even Percy the painter, for once found themselves at one when it came to the question of choosing between the danger of being looked in at and the delight of looking out over a pastoral scene. To these worthies it is unthinkable that privacy should be threatened by aesthetic considerations, and much obstinate argument, petering out into the dumb protest of shoulder shrugging, preceded their final surrender. It seems common heresy, not only to those who treasure privacy, but to the many others who read, write, and think in a smallest room, that one should so arrange things as to obtain an agreeable outlook notwithstanding the presence of bookshelves, pictures, and a well-chosen scheme of soothing decoration.

Nevertheless, it must be emphasized that the view shall be congenial and not one to arouse such emotions as fear or the vertigo experienced by an acquaintance of Reginald Reynolds in Norway: '. . . he had occasion to pass a night in a *saeta*, where he arrived after dark. And being moved to relieve himself after he had breakfasted, he sought the house of office, where he was about to seat himself when he was astonished to spy daylight through the hole beneath him. Looking downwards, he was horrified to discover that the place overhung a precipice of some 2,000 feet, and that he was looking into the distant waters of a *fjord*, where a large ship appeared as a small object framed in the *chaise percée* (like the picture of Queen Victoria which an ignorant artisan framed in like manner, thinking so fine a piece of polished wood could hardly have been intended for so base a use). When I enquired of this person what were his reactions, he replied that his principal desire was to feel his feet upon terra firma, and that he therefore withdrew in haste from the place without attempting to transact his affairs. But surely, said I, such places were expressly devised to precipitate business by the emotion of fear, which may well have proved a stronger and cheaper medicine than *Enos*, and account for the excellent health of the Norwegians. To this, however, my friend only replied that he would sooner suffer from habitual costiveness than expose himself daily to such peril and to a matutinal fantasy of breaking timber swaying over such an abyss, however much it might *encourager les autres.*'

For the most happily expressed aesthetic enjoyment of a smallest room, I must refer again to Gwen Raverat, describing the home of her grandfather Charles Darwin: 'And just as everything else at Down was perfect, so there too was the most beautiful, secret, romantic lavatory that ever was known; at the end of a long passage and up several steps. It had the only window which looked out over the orchard, and was always full of a dim green light. You looked down into the tops of the apple trees; and when I read *Romeo and Juliet* (which was the first Shakespeare I read for myself) the line "That tips with silver all these fruit-tree tops," always made me think of that window.'

By no means least among the pleasures of the smallest room are those afforded by the manufacturers of sanitary ware. There are the actual names, such as Twyford, Shanks, Crapper, Froy, Jennings, Doulton, suddenly encountered in the most remote and unlikely places, to offer a special reassurance to the traveller. After all, we tell ourselves, with Anglo-Saxon complacency, things cannot be too bad if such people as these have blazed their hygienic trail. It may even be surmised that some such feelings mingled with the conviviality of Lord Beaverbrook and members of his Mission to Moscow during the Second World War when, after what was described as a 'slap-up' party with the late Comrade Stalin, they discovered the Kremlin toilet to be by Shanks. That the British were active pioneers in the smallest rooms of Tzarist Russia is now a matter for a nostalgic satisfaction. A passing glimpse of the heyday of this trade is afforded by Joseph Hatton's account of a visit to Thomas William Twyford, who in 1887 founded his great works in the potteries. Hatton at the turn of the century described him as 'fresh from one of his tours of business and pleasure through France and Germany to St. Petersburg and Moscow.'

The inventiveness of manufacturers is a never-failing source of pleasure to the curious visiting the smallest rooms of others. It seems reasonable enough that Messrs. Crapper should name some of their works *The Deluge*, *The Torrent*, *The Rapidus*, or even *The Rocket*, but what flights of fancy or political allies are, I wonder, responsible for *The Zone*, *The Axis*, *The Cardinal*, and *The Orion*?

I must here resist the temptation urged on me by several men of letters to quote more freely from this poetry of the smallest room. I have been offered many curious and fanciful examples, and at one time I considered printing them as an appendix. My researches, however, persuaded me that this would be an unsportsmanlike act. I have encountered an eminent musician, several legal luminaries and politicians, authors of several nationalities, and many able men and women engaged in commerce whose hobby it is to collect such names. It is a point of honour with them that they shall have discovered curious names for themselves—and indeed used them. Like all collectors, they are ardent in their blameless and diverting pursuit, even if they are, like school-boys, boastful of their achievement, furtively given to swops. It would be the act of a spoil-sport to publish my own collection to which many of them have so generously contributed.

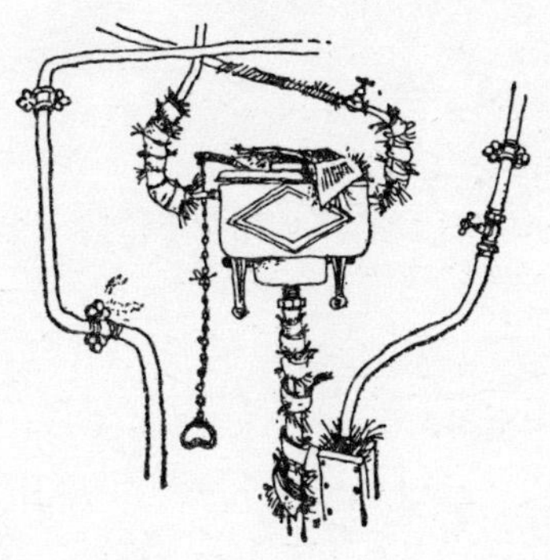

Sir John Harington—Pioneer

HARINGTON, THE INVENTOR OF THE ENGLISH W.C.—HIS TELEVISION APPEARANCE—HIS STORY—HIS 'AJAX'—HIS RELATIONSHIP TO QUEEN ELIZABETH I—HIS EIGHTEENTH-CENTURY SUCCESSORS—THE INAUGURATION OF OUR OWN SMALLEST ROOM

IT is a pleasing thought that the inventor of that device we now take for granted as the focal comfort of all our smallest rooms, the water-closet, was a man of letters; a poet and one to whom the first Queen Elizabeth referred as 'that witty fellow, my godson.'

It was, moreover, a pleasing and welcome lapse from the public prudery of this other Elizabethan age that the B.B.C. Television Service presented the witty fellow in person to demonstrate his device in the course of an Elizabethan version of their Society of Inventors programme. He came before our eyes with the announcement: 'We welcome to the Society this evening Master John Harington, the famous courtier and scholar. He has brought us his model of a new privy.'

He was then probed, as are modern inventors, by the ever-inquiring mind of Geoffrey Boumphrey:

BOUMPHREY: Good evening, Master Harington. We are very interested to know how you came to invent this strange contraption.

HARINGTON: My reading of ancient records and histories gave me the notion. I discovered that the great magistrates of the past have employed their wits, their care, and their costs in devising such inventions. I thought it provident to revive some of their ideas which have been hidden these many years. I conceived this device because it was rather a pleasure than a pain; a matter so slight that it will seem at the first incredible, so sure that you shall find it at all times infallible. It does avoid at once all the annoyances that can be imagined.

BOUMPHREY: Is this the first invention you have designed?

HARINGTON: Yes, alas. I am not much given to working with my hands.

BOUMPHREY: Was it not a long time in the making, Master Harington?

HARINGTON: Yes, several years. I have had the advice of masons and workers in metal to help me complete my task.

BOUMPHREY: Will it please you to show us how it works?

There followed the demonstration of a clever imitation of this father of all our water-closets, a lively piece of reconstruction and a pioneering performance of some significance, in that it surely marked the first appearance of any W.C. on any television screen. Afterwards the Tudor view of these things was nicely expressed thus:

BOUMPHREY: I do much admire your invention, Master Harington. What a conception! You should be much praised for hitting on it. Yet, if you consider, there are only three privies in the whole of Tower Street, for the services of sixty-five houses. There seems small chance of your device being taken into general use.

HARINGTON: You speak truth, Master Boumphrey. We are barbarians in England. I doubt that few of Her Majesty's subjects would deem it worth while to install such an expensive invention.

In this one essay into practical invention, John Harington was well ahead of his time; but in other respects, robustly enough, to his own age.

He was one of a family which derived its name from Haverington in Cumberland. The fortunes of the Haringtons became involved with the issues of the Wars of the Roses. It was Sir James Harington who took Henry VI captive and dispatched him to the Tower and subsequent death, for which he was granted lands by Edward IV. In 1485 he fought on the side of crookbacked Richard at Bosworth and hence, after the accession of Henry VII, was attainted and those lands were presumably included in the twenty-five manors which he was compelled to forfeit to the Crown. After the death of Sir James, and that of his childless son, the claim to the lost lands passed to his brother, Sir Robert, whose son, another James, entered the Church and became Dean of York. The grandson of the dean was John Harington of Stepney, father of our hero.

John Harington of Stepney revived the family's fortunes. He went to Court, held a succession of important offices, and became treasurer of the king's camps and buildings. About 1546 he married Etheldreda Malte, a byblow of the lusty Henry VIII by Joanna Dyngley, discreetly brought up by the king's tailor, John Malte, as a natural daughter of his own. Etheldreda brought her husband manors in Somerset granted her by the king, including that of Kelston, which was destined to become the birthplace of the W.C. in the lifetime of her stepson, for she, alas, died without issue but a year after her marriage, leaving her lands to her husband.

John Harington, the young widower, seems to have been a man of some culture. A handful of poems by him are still extant and, in 1550, he published *The Booke of Freendeship*, a translation of Cicero's *De Amicitia*. He attached himself to the cause of the young princess Elizabeth and shared some of her tribulations during the reign of her sister Mary. He visited her in her captivity at Hatfield and gallantly wrote verses to all her six gentlewomen but singled out, for especial admiration, Isabella, daughter of Sir John Markham of Cotham. Isabella became his second wife and shared his eleven-months' imprisonment in the Tower, to which he was committed in 1554, for having secretly conveyed a letter to Elizabeth.

Four years later Mary was dead, and with Elizabeth I on the throne all was well with the Haringtons. About 1561 a son, John, our hero, was born and the queen rewarded his parents' loyalty by standing as the child's godmother. Nor was this an empty compliment. When the lad was at Eton, she sent him a copy of a speech she made to Parliament in March, 1575, with a letter: 'Boye Jacke, I have made a clerke wryte faire my poore wordes for thyne use. . . . Ponder theme in thy howres of leysure, and plaie wythe theme tyll they enter thyne understandinge; . . . and I do thys, because thy father was readye to serve and love us in trouble and thrall. . . .'

Courtiers followed where the queen led. Afterwards, at King's College, Cambridge, John received a letter from the great Lord Burleigh offering him good advice about his undergraduate career, and signed 'Your fathers frende that loves you.' Harington stayed up until 1581 when he graduated. Later in life he reproached himself that he had played 'the scholar and students part too negligently.' Yet he must somehow have come by the store of wide general learning that he was to show in his writings, and, it is possible, to please a father who saw in it a way to preferment, that he may have begun to read law at Cambridge.

At all events, after he had taken his degree, he entered the Inns of Court as a member of Lincoln's Inn. But it was as an eager wit and as a gay young man of the world, that his reputation began to be established. Court favour understandably seemed a pleasanter way of advancement than legal assiduity during the year or so before his father died and he came into his inheritance.

It was farewell to the law then, and to bachelor life. He married Mary Rogers, daughter of the widowed Lady Rogers, a Somerset neighbour, and they settled down to live at Kelston. They may then have discussed plans for building a fine new house, for Harington was seldom averse to spending money. But, though his estates claimed some of his time and, in 1584, he was appointed a justice of the peace, John Harington could never long keep away from Court. There his liveliness and wit were welcome, and his epigrams had an increasing circulation, either in manuscript or by word of mouth.

But wit over-reached itself. For the amusement of the ladies of the Court, he translated the story of Giacondo from the twenty-eighth book of Ariosto's *Orlando Furioso.* This scandalous piece concerns two cuckolds, who, by way of avenging themselves, set out to seduce every woman they come across. Then, wearying, they set up a joint mistress, in the hope that she may be faithful to two when none are capable of a simple and single fidelity. Again they are disappointed and so return to their wives, recognizing that, after all, they are as chaste and honest as the rest. The maids-of-honour were much taken with this sally. The manuscript went round. Soon it fell into the hands of the queen. She was furious, or pretended to be. She accused the poet of attempting to corrupt the morals of her ladies. But there was possibly a deeper implication. Her own chastity was a factor in foreign relations and a reflection on the chastity of women in general by her own godson might have repercussions. She could not overlook the affair. Harington must be punished. The punishment should fit the crime. He had translated part of one book of his original. Very well then. He should be banished Court and must return to Kelston until he had translated all the forty-six books of Ariosto's poem. Harington went.

He returned. In 1591 he triumphantly published a great folio containing the entire *Orlando Furioso* in free translation with 'An Epistle Dedicatorie to the Queenes Majestie,' and, for good measure, an allegory of the whole poem, a life of Ariosto, a critical essay—*An Apologie of Poetrie*, and notes. The folio also contains an engraved frontispiece containing a portrait of the translator, one of the four likenesses that survive and serve to confirm our estimate of his personal appearance. We see an alert face, the cheekbones somewhat high, bright eyes under arched brows, the hair, full at the sides, growing to a peak on the forehead, a well-shaped mouth, and a small pointed beard. And a nose, something tip-tilted, and sensitive.

Yes, a sensitive nose, a nose competent to concern itself with problems of cleanliness. He had indeed been brought up in a tradition concerned with such matters. His father had devised, in 1566, some 'Orders for Household Servantes,' in which it was laid down 'That no man make water within either of the courts, upon pain of, every time it shall be proved, one penny,' and Harington was to renew these a year or two later.

That sensitive nose of his indeed informed him

sharply enough that such orders were no real attempt to solve the problems posed by Tudor standards of manners and sanitation. While occupied in his epic task of translation, he was also busy rebuilding Kelston from an Italian design by Barozzi of Vignola. We do not know exactly what the new house was like, for it was pulled down in the mid-eighteenth century. From references to pictures, walks, and ponds, and to a 'fountain on pillars, under which you may dine and sup,' it must have been a pleasant place. What, however, made it different from all other Elizabethan houses was its smallest room.

I like to think that he discussed it all with some Elizabethan west-country prototype of Mr. Fleet, that there was that sort of give-and-take of ideals and practicability. Yet it seems to have taken a more highfalutin level, as he later recorded it. 'The device was both first thought of, and discoursed of, with as broad terms as any belongs to it, in presence of six persons . . . of which, I was so much the meanest, in that the other five, for beauty, for birth, for value, for wit, and for wealth, are not in many places of the realm to be matched . . . in a castle, that I call the wonder of the west.' What a subject for an imaginary conversation, for a mural in some grand public place!

Neither Harington nor his fine company esconced in the wonder of the west had any inkling, I suppose, of the domestic wonder their talk was helping to create. His own thoughts were perhaps more given to the publication of his *Orlando*.

With all the eagerness of authors of every degree,

he waited on its reception. Nothing very much happened. Disillusioned, he kicked his heels at Kelston, perhaps a little solaced by his appointment as high sheriff of Somerset in 1592, an honour that cost him dear as it fell to his lot to entertain the queen on her visit to Bath that year. Perhaps Her Majesty was introduced to the smallest room at Kelston. In any case, as time went by, the comfort and convenience of his new device became increasingly apparent to Harington himself and he determined to make it serve the purpose of his ambitions. He would write a 'fantastical treatise' about it. 'I was the willinger to wryte such a toye as this,' he says, 'because I had layne me thought allmost buryed in the Contry these three or fowre yeares, and I thought this would give some occasion to have me thought of and talked of.'

Richard Field, who had published *Orlando*, also put out this shorter work with a longer title, *A New Discourse of a Stale Subject; Called the Metamorphosis of Ajax, Written by Misacmos to his Friend and Cousin Philostilpnos.*

The book is prefaced by a letter purporting to be 'written by a Gentleman of Good Worth to the Author of the Book,' in which he claims to have heard much of Kelston and particularly of the little room as being as 'sweet as my parlour.' He therefore entreats the author 'to set down the manner of it in writing . . . or to cause your man . . . make a draught or plot thereof.' In this way 'you should make many of your friends much beholding to you; and perhaps you might cause reformation in many houses that

. . . will think it no scorn to follow your good example. Nay, to tell you my opinion seriously, if you have so easy, so cheap, and so infallible a way for avoiding such annoyances in great houses, you may not only pleasure many great persons but do her Majesty good Service in her Palace of Greenwich and other stately houses, that are oft annoyed with such savours as where many mouths be fed can hardly be avoided. Also you might be a great benefactor to the City of London and all other populous towns, who stand in great need of such conveyances.'

Then, of course, follows *The Answer to the Letter*, in which the author Misacmos (which, I am told, is Greek for 'hater of filth') deprecates an interest in 'the basest room of my house,' but nevertheless suggests that he is 'so wholly addicted to her highness's "service" ' that if his invention should 'effect so good a reformation in the palace of Richmond or Greenwich' an appointment as one of the privy chamber would come suitably pat.

The three main sections of the book itself are first 'to justify the use of the homeliest words in so necessary matters'; second 'to prove the matter not to be contemptible'; and third 'to shew the form, and how it may be reformed.' All three are written with gusto, with a lively display of learning farced with anecdote and quotation, and with some political allusions that escape us now and would have been better omitted then.

The first section affords us a pleasant glimpse inside the smallest room at Kelston, for Harington prints a verse and gives a woodcut illustration of what he calls 'a homely emblem . . . set up in Cloacina's chapel at my house.' The picture shows a seated clergyman to whom the devil has appeared. The verse runs:

> A godly Father, sitting on a draught,
> To doe as need, and Nature hath vs taught,
> Mumbled, as was his manner, certaine prayers:
> And vnto him, the Diuell straight repaires,
> And boldly to reuile him he begins,
> Alleaging, that such prayers are deadly sinnes;
> And that it prou'd he was deuoyd of grace,
> To speake to God in so vnfit a place.
> The reuerend man, though at the first dismayd,
> Yet strong in faith, thus to the Diuell said:
> Thou damned Spirit, wicked, false, and lying,
> Despayring thine owne good, and our enuying:
> Each take his due, and me thou canst not hurt,
> To God my prayer I meant, to thee the durt.
> Pure prayer ascends to him that high doth sit.
> Downe falls the filth, for fiends of hell more fit.

At the close, the author indulges in a defence of the style he has adopted for his book, inquiring of the reader with a modesty which seems mostly absent from our own times, if he had been more grave and sober, 'would you have ever asked for the book?' He then produces a punning moral:

> To keep your houses sweet, cleanse privy vaults:
> To keep your souls as sweet, mend privy faults—

and with that writes 'Finis.'

It is not the end though. The Gentleman of Good Worth had suggested in his preliminary letter that there should be illustrations of the contrivance. So there is a practical appendix: 'An Anatomy of the

Metamorpho-sed Ajax . . . Published for the Common Benefit of Builders, Housekeepers, and House-Owners,' supposititiously by T.C.

This T.C. was Harington's man—a rustic predecessor of our own Mr. Fleet, though no doubt more servile, but with a tongue in his head notwithstanding and a will of his own when it came to a choice of adjectives. 'My master having expressly commanded me to finish a strange discourse . . . by setting certain pictures thereto,' he writes, flourishing two woodcuts before us. Of the first, showing all the separate component parts, he explains: 'This is Don AJAX house of the new fashion, all in sunder . . .' His second depicts the assembled contraption with (delightful touch!) little fishes swimming in the cistern. An itemized schedule of costs for everything, except the fishes, is then presented, by which it appears that the whole should not cost more than thirty shillings and eightpence—but then, as Mr. Fleet hastened to point out when we mentioned this modest sum, several wars have happened since then, and somebody has to pay for them.

Harington's book precipitated a ding-dong pamphlet warfare. He may have helped to foster this in the hopes of compelling notice for his ideas, although the *Ulysses Upon Ajax* avers that his 'use of hydraulic engines' was not his own notion but 'borrowed from Vitruvius, or else taken . . . from a traveller's mouth who hath seen the Cardinal of Ferrara's buildings at Tivoli.' This is as may be. Certainly, the idea, adopted or original, was being discussed. The Queen was amused, and interested. Harington's eyes brightened at the prospect of fulfilled ambition. Then the blow fell. It was pointed out to Elizabeth that one of her godson's shafts was aimed at the memory of Leicester, her dead favourite. There was no mistaking her anger now. Even the Star Chamber was talked of. A licence was refused for printing the book, though three editions had appeared. The hapless Harington was once more forbidden Court 'till he had grown sober.'

Once more, however, he was forgiven. Among the hundreds of Harington's epigrams we find one 'To the Queen when she was pacified, and had sent Misacmos thanks for the inuention.' She had realized that underlying the fripperies of the author's style was a serious intention—'the marrow of the book'—and she put it to the proof. She caused one of the new devices to be installed at Richmond Palace, with a copy of the *Ajax* depending from the wall. Inevitably an epigram followed. 'To the Ladies of the Queenes Priuy-Chamber, at the making of their perfumed priuy at *Richmond*, The Booke hanged in chaines saith thus:

Faire Dames, if any tooke in scorne, and spite
Me, that *Misacmos* Muse in mirth did write,
To satisfie the sinne, loe, here in chaines,
For aye to hang, my Master me ordaines.
Yet deeme the deed to him no derogation,
But deign to this deuice new commendation,
Sith here you see, feele, smell that his conueyance
Hath freed this noysome place from all annoyance.
Now iudge you, that the work mock, enuie, taunt,
Whose seruice in this place may make most vaunt:
  If vs, or you, to praise it, were most meet,
  You, that made sowre, or vs, that make it sweet?'

Yet this petty success—little more than a flush in the pan—was so much less than Harington had hoped for and he was compelled to be content with family pleasures and the country delights of Kelston—'my Mall, my childrene, and my cattle, all well fedde, well taughte, and well belovede.' His zeal for sanitary reform may well have contributed to the then exceptional fact that seven of his nine children survived their infancy.

No more conspicuous employment than the quiet pursuits of a scholarly country gentleman seem to have been afforded Harington until 1599, when the Earl of Essex was sent on his ill-fated expedition against the Irish rebels. Essex wrote to Harington that the Queen herself had 'specially commended yourselfe to my assistance and notyse.' Battle training, it seemed, was not a factor of importance in those warlike days and Harington was appointed commander of horse under the Earl of Southampton. In addition to the normal hazards of fighting, Harington's position was made politically invidious by reason of the Court-feuds between the Essex and the Cecils. Before the departure of the expedition, he was warned by his cousin to dissemble 'that damnable uncovered honesty of yours. . . . Obey the Lord Deputy in all things, but give not your opinion; it may be heard in England.' Caution, induced by his cousin's counsel, prompted him to keep a journal of events in Ireland, but caution was over-ruled by vanity when he allowed himself to be one of the eighty-one knights created by Essex, a stretch of authority that added to the Queen's already formidable anger at the disasters of the expedition. Summoned to London, Essex brought Harington with him, perhaps hoping thereby to stem the old Queen's wrath. 'What,' she stormed, when Harington knelt in her presence, 'did the foole brynge *you* too? Go backe to your businesse,' and the new knight fled to Kelston, he says, as if all the Irish rebels had been at his heels.

Yet he was at Court again when his former leader Essex himself rebelled in 1601. Though Harington proved himself a staunch Queen's-man, the almost-seventy-years-old Elizabeth was increasingly irascible and again dismissed him with: 'It is no season now to foole it here.' She was approaching her end and was out of humour with that witty fellow her godson. Once, in her last days, when he had read some verses to her, she said: 'When thou doste feele creepinge tyme at thye gate, these fooleries will please thee lesse.'

With a capacity for free-spending and the claims of a large family to consider, it is not surprising that Harington, in the face of unrewarded ambition, should turn fortune-hunter, with an eye particularly to the estate of his mother-in-law, Lady Rogers. His brother-in-law, Edward Rogers, was naturally a resolute rival and resented attempts to persuade the old lady to disinherit her son in favour of her daughter, Harington's wife. The two of them were at loggerheads as early as 1594 when Rogers boasted of having pulled out a handful of his brother-in-law's beard as he was leaving Westminster Hall. When Lady Rogers lay dying in January 1602, exhausted by wrangling and importunity, Harington entered the house, broke open chests, and endeavoured to secure possession. On her death, he refused to yield possession and a Star Chamber suit was brought against him and he ran the risk of imprisonment.

He was at liberty during the last days of Elizabeth, of which he left us an interesting account, when, like many another, he set himself to gain the favours of her probable successor, James VI of Scotland. To that end, he sent his royal fellow-poet and scholar a new-year's gift of a curiously constructed lantern, intended to symbolize the waning light of Elizabeth and the noonday glory of the splendour that was to come with James and bearing a representation of the crucifixion, for the sake of an almost-blasphemous introduction of the words of the impenitent thief: 'Lord, remember me when thou comest into thy kingdom.' Harington also prepared a treatise 'On the Succession to the Throne.' Ill-luck dogged him, however, and he had no opportunity of presenting this. When James entered London, our hero, having become involved in another lawsuit, was in prison for debt.

On his release he sought and, at last, was granted an interview with James. The talk turned on witchcraft. 'Sir John,' said the King, 'do you truly understand why the Devil works more with ancient women than others?' Unwarned by the King's gravity, Harington 'could not refrain from a scurvy jest,' and it was his undoing. Once again, opportunity was lost.

Nevertheless, our witty fellow wore a good thick skin. When, in 1605, Archbishop Loftus died, thereby leaving two offices vacant, that of Archbishop of Dublin and Lord Chancellor of Ireland, Harington promptly offered himself for both. Cecil ignored the application. Harington undaunted began to angle for a tutorship to the young prince Henry. At last he was given some share in the education of the prince and from there on seems to have been a person of some little consequence about the Court. But his health began to fail. In May 1612 we find him at Kelston 'sicke of a dead palsie.' In the following November, aged 51, he died.

His memory was kept alive not by his pioneer work in the smallest room, but by the epigrams which in his own lifetime were sometimes cherished, sometimes feared. His reputation may be judged by an anecdote preserved in Fuller's *Worthies:* 'It happened that while the said Sir John repaired often to an ordinary in Bath, a female attendress at the table, neglecting other gentlemen which sat higher, and were of greater estates, applied herself wholly to him, accommodating him with all necessaries, and preventing his asking anything with her officiousness. She, being demanded of him the reason of her so careful waiting on him: "I understand," said she, "you are a very witty man, and if I should displease you in anything, I fear you would make an epigram of me." '

After his death, these epigrams which almost every occasion in his life had prompted, were first printed. A grandson published a manuscript on the characters of the Elizabethan bishops which he had written for Prince Henry's use. Some of his letters and papers were published in the eighteenth century by a descendant. Other things have come to light and have been printed since. But Harington's name is for the most part now only remembered by scholars and specialists—but for his brief glory as a televised pioneer. His *Ajax* was reprinted in 1814 and in 1927. His lasting memorial is the ceaseless sound of the water music of the world's smallest rooms, a broadcast which is never stilled.

He was indeed ahead of his time as a practical benefactor of his fellow-men. Minoan civilization fourteen hundred years before Christ in matters of wholesome sanitation was far in advance of that of Britain even in the eighteenth century when Alexander Cumming, a Bond Street watchmaker, took out the first patent for a water-closet. If this was an offspring of the inventive genius of John Harington it was, in 1775, a most tardy acknowledgment, coming well over a century and a half after our hero's death. The valve closet of Joseph Bramah, a cabinet maker, was the next patent, in 1778: and, vitally important, the first patent for a stink-trap taken out in 1782 by John Gaillait, a cook.

Observe that no plumber could claim any part of the glory of these early inventive exploits. It took first the creative impulse of a poet, our hero Harington: then the meticulous skill of a watchmaker, the practical mind of a cabinet-maker, and finally the flair of a cook. Yet we decided, on balance, that it should be Mr. Fleet who should perform the opening ceremony when at length our chaste, so thoughtfully planned and furnished tribute to Cloacina was ready for use. The invitation took him by surprise and at first filled him with confusion.

'What me go in there with everybody listening outside?' said he, delicately assuming that shade of purple which we have learnt to recognize as a blush.

In the end we settled for a rendering of 'For he's a jolly good fellow' to drown any possible embarrassment occasioned by the sounds of the opening ceremony and the first flushing that completed the gambit.

Toward the end of this anthem which admittedly may have seemed startling if not meaningless to anyone passing by, unaware of the significance of the occasion, a personage making an effort to conceal his surprise, with an air of official decorum joined us. To Mr. Fleet emerging, pleased and purple, from the still musical waters of the smallest room, this personage said: 'I am from the Local Authority. The application for planning permission to erect a small building on this site has been referred back and disallowed . . .'

Mr. Fleet went a very deep purple. 'Shall we pull it all down, or shall we just lock him in till he comes to himself?' he said.

PUBLIC
CONVENIENCES
BOROUGH OF
THE LORD NELSON
LADI
ALES
USE
GENTLEMEN
FOR WHITER WOOLIES
DRESSING ROOM
HOT & COLD WATER
WITH USE OF CLEAN
TOWELS & BRUSH
2
LADIES